Safe Haven

Safe Haven

Ellen Hoil

Desert Palm Press

Safe Haven

by Ellen Hoil

© 2006, 2019 Ellen Hoil

ISBN-(book) 9781948327442
ISBN-(epub) 9781948327459
ISBN (pdf) 9781948327466

Desert Palm Press
1961 Main Street, Suite 220
Watsonville, California 95076
www.desertpalmpress.com

Editor: Mary Hettel
Cover Design: TreeHouse Studio

Printed in the United States of America
First Edition October 2019

Acknowledgement

For the all the people who have helped me with this over the years I am truly grateful.

To Mary O'Connell who acted as my first editor all those years ago, and to my two most recent ones, Mary and Glenda, I am eternally grateful. All three of you have taught me a great deal about this wonderful craft called writing.

Amy Tee, though she had no part in the writing, has shown me over the years how important it is to fight stigma every moment of every day. Every day people struggle through the most basic tasks fighting not only the illness, but also the stigma society places on them.

For those interested in learning more, please visit The National Alliance on Mental Illness at www.nami.org

DEDICATION

To Mary Adolfo and Wizzy Boo, who first believed I had a story in me to tell, and to Tacey and Michelle for helping me learn to be me. For all of those living with the stigma of mental illness, know you are heard.

Chapter One

BRIGID WATCHED AS THE woman moved past the window, reading as she walked. She would pass the store every two hours or so, her head always down, buried in her book. It appeared the woman didn't notice anything around her. Something about the woman resonated with Brigid. *How can anybody read and walk without bumping into things? What is she reading that is so engrossing?*

The woman was already walking each morning when Brigid opened her shop and was still there when she went home at night. She began timing the sightings and noticed they came with a general regularity. She could set her watch by when the woman passed the window. Every forty minutes—about the amount of time it took her to walk from one end of town to the other.

She didn't think the woman was homeless. She appeared clean, and well-kept every day. But the only possession she carried was her book. The woman looked like she could use a few extra meals. Brigid never saw her with food. She wondered if the woman ate at all and would be more worried if the weather wasn't so warm. *Does she just keep going? What does she do at night? She must sleep and clean up somewhere.*

The time Brigid stood at the front window to catch a glimpse of the woman wasn't much of an interference. The small bookshop was slow this time of year. The droves of summer tourists had yet to arrive and the locals tended to come by in the late afternoon or evening. Her staff didn't work until then, so she found herself standing in front of the glass windows, watching for the woman. The need to work finally drove her from her vigil.

The day the woman's routine changed was a beautiful spring day, cool enough to enjoy, but warm enough to remind that summer was fast approaching. Brigid tried to do her work, but she was sidetracked every time someone walked by the window and it wasn't the woman. Brigid checked her watch. It was over two hours since the last time the woman passed the store. Brigid felt as though a lunch date had stood her up.

Looking out Brigid saw the familiar blonde down the street sitting on one the benches in front of the deli. From where Brigid stood, it looked as if the stranger was just staring at nothing, just looking into some far-off point. Her book was open on her lap, but she wasn't looking down at the pages. Brigid watched her for several minutes, thinking at some moment she would resume her walk. Brigid thought that maybe she might go into the deli and get some food, or go to the park to read, but the woman didn't move, she merely sat and continued to stare. She sat so still that from where Brigid was watching, she couldn't see the woman making any movement. After twenty minutes, curiosity got the best of Brigid and she put up the "out to lunch" sign. As she walked to the deli, Brigid glanced at the woman as she passed behind her. The stranger didn't move or give any indication that she had noticed Brigid enter the delicatessen.

"Hi, Brigid." Steve said from behind the display case.

"Hi, Steve. How are Taylor and the baby?"

Steve's smile grew. "They're doing great. Kid is growing like a weed."

Brigid chuckled at how excited Steve was. Steve went on for a few minutes about the perfections of his new baby. However, Brigid's mind quickly returned to her reason for coming in and began to ask Steve about the strange woman.

"She's been spending a lot of time here on Main Street."

"Yeah, I've noticed that. How could you miss her? The woman's like a machine." Steve said, shaking his head.

Brigid rummaged through the soda case. "Has she ever stopped in for anything?" She placed two cans on the counter.

"No, she hasn't. Now that you mention it that is a bit weird, since my place is the only one nearby to grab a quick bite from."

"Hmmm, that is interesting. I wonder what she's doing for food." Brigid ran her hand through her hair deep in thought.

"So, what can I get you today?" Steve asked as other customers entered the deli.

"How about a large Italian hero?" Brigid said.

Steve gave her a knowing wink. "Sure."

Once the hero and drinks were in her hands, Brigid headed for the door. "Thanks for the lunch, big guy. Tell Taylor I'll stop by around two o'clock," she said as she opened the door.

"Will do."

The woman still sat on the bench, as a tree a few feet away let the sunshine peek through the leaves and shine on her. This was the first close look Brigid had of her. The light flickered through the wind-blown leaves and accented her blonde hair. She noticed the woman did seem in need of a haircut. What she assumed was once a neat short cut, had grown in, leaving an uneven line across the base of her neck and over her ears. From where she stood just a few feet away, Brigid could see the hair was also well past her eyes. Brigid watched as the woman ran her hand through it to move it off her face.

Brigid gathered up her courage and, as she stepped in front of the bench, she cleared her throat to get the woman's attention. When that failed, she tried a more direct manner. "Hi. Is this seat taken?"

Brigid was only a little surprised when there was no response. She sat down and placed the large sandwich between them. She sat slightly facing the blonde and began eating her lunch. The woman continued to stare across the street.

Brigid now had an unobstructed view of the woman's profile. She had angular features, high cheekbones with a long sharp jaw line and a straight nose. Her face had a healthy tan from her hours outside. The woman's beauty reminded her of the movie *Sabrina* with Audrey Hepburn. A hidden beauty in a simple package.

As she munched on half of the sandwich, Brigid tried to see the woman's eyes. From what she could see, they were a deep cerulean blue. At first glance, the woman appeared to stare ahead with a blank expression. However, Brigid noticed that her eyes were constantly moving. Brigid also noticed a slight tremor in the woman's hands as she held her closed book. The hands were sleek and muscular, the tendons strained from her tight grip.

The woman's leg jiggled to the rhythm of an imagined beat. It seemed to take all of the woman's concentration to sit for this little bit of time. It was similar to a caged animal as it paced within its cage hoping to find itself free if the tiger paced hard enough and long enough. Brigid didn't understand why it did, but the similarity made her sad.

"Excuse me?" Brigid asked.

The woman turned to Brigid as if she hadn't realized Brigid was sitting next to her. The woman's jaw muscle clenched, and an emotion Brigid couldn't place flashed in the blonde's eyes. Brigid waited for a response but there was none. A pleading look passed over the woman's eyes as she turned back around. The look passed and was replaced again with fear.

"I was hoping you could help me. I know this will sound stupid, but I'm less hungry than I thought, and I can't finish this half of the hero." Brigid pointed at the sandwich. "If you could finish it for me. I hate to waste food. I'll even throw in a soda to sweeten the deal." Brigid set the soda on the bench next to the sandwich.

The woman turned toward Brigid, and then without a word, she resumed her stare across the street, her eyes moving quickly back and forth, as if trying to take in the whole scene in one moment.

"Please, it would make me feel better rather than throw it out. I work over there and I promise I'm not some kind of weird serial poisoner roaming the streets to kill people with sandwiches." Brigid pointed to her store.

Without making eye contact, the corners of the woman's mouth twitched slightly upward. Brigid waited several moments for an answer, but there was none. She left the soda and sandwich on the bench as she stood to leave.

"Well, if you want it, it's right here. I wish you would enjoy it."

As Brigid walked back to the store, she was annoyed that she had gotten nowhere with the woman. The bell over the door jingled as she slammed it in frustration. She hadn't expected much but had hoped for it anyway. She went to the window to see what the woman was doing.

The blonde sat staring straight ahead. But once in a while she would turn and look at the leftover sandwich. Brigid watched her for nearly ten minutes until the woman finally picked up the hero. She ate it faster than Brigid had ever seen anyone eat before. The woman ravaged her lunch in three large bites. She opened her book and then, just as quietly as she stopped, she began her walk again.

Chapter Two

FOR THE NEXT TWO WEEKS, the woman sat on the bench at lunchtime. After the first day, Brigid bought an extra hero and soda. She would sit on the bench with the woman as she ate, and then leave the extras there. When Brigid left, the woman would look at the food for a minute or two, tuck her book under her arm, and take the meal.

"You still feeding the stray?" Brigid's employee, Melissa said as she looked over her shoulder and out the window. "You know, just because you feed them doesn't mean you can keep them, and I'm not taking care of it if you bring it home. I bet she sheds."

Melissa was one of Brigid's closest friends. So, Brigid recognized the tone of teasing in her voice. "Have you seen how fast she eats those sandwiches? I wonder if she eats anything else. She looks like a rail. I'd swear she's lost fifteen pounds since she showed up here."

"Yeah, well, she does get a lot of exercise."

Ignoring the barb, Brigid turned to her. "I suppose."

"So, are you going to stand here all day, or are you going to help me put away the new shipment of books?"

"I'm coming. Did we get deliveries from all the vendors?" Brigid followed Melissa to the storeroom.

"Yeah, they all came. Including the new book, I've been sniffing after." Melissa rubbed her hands together.

"Now will you stop bothering me about it?" Brigid grinned at her friend.

"Yes. Rita was asking for it." Melissa's demeanor perked up at the mention of her partner's name.

Brigid and Melissa spent the rest of the afternoon emptying boxes, shelving books, and assisting customers. After two hours of quiet, the bell over the door announced a new customer. Brigid looked up to see Mrs. Kendrick and her four and a half-year-old daughter, Laura, entering the store. Brigid put down the book she was about to shelve and headed up the aisle to meet them by the children's corner. The area was set up with little tables and chairs so the kids could sit and look at the books. Brigid felt it made them feel as if they were in control of their decision to buy a book.

"Hi, Laura. How are you today?"

"Hi, Miss Brigid. Mom said we can get a book today because I did a good job at piano lessons. I played the song all the way," the pig-tailed girl said.

Brigid got down on one knee to be on the girl's level. "Well, that certainly is a big thing, Laura, and I agree that does deserve a prize. Did you have a book in mind?"

"We thought, maybe, another Beatrix Potter," Mrs. Kendrick said.

"Yeah, I want Mrs. Tittlemouse," Laura said as she clapped her hands.

"Well, why don't you see if you can find it? It will be on the shelf marked 'P.' Do you know which one that is?" Brigid pointed to the general area.

"It's the one with Pooh on it," Laura said.

"You're very right and so very smart." Brigid said, giving a little clap.

Laura smiled and scampered to the corner.

Mrs. Kendrick looked after her daughter. "She really has fallen in love with those Beatrix Potter books, Brigid. Thanks for showing them to her. I wonder sometimes if she isn't trying to be more and more like Benjamin Bunny and Tom Kitten. I've never seen one of my kids get into so much mischief. The other day I caught her trying to turn her little brother into a roly-poly pudding." She chuckled. "She had him on the floor wrapped in some string she found. I had to use scissors to get him out of it."

"Well, at least she didn't get the pie crust on him."

"You're right. By the way, when will you have the book mobile at the school?"

"It's planned for next Friday. I'd like to give the kids some books to start the summer off with."

Brigid held the school's book fair every year. She sold the books to the children at cost so that some of the less fortunate ones could afford to own a new book. The money was donated to a local cause the children picked. This year the money was going to the local animal shelter to help foster the animals out to families.

"Thank you, Brigid. I know the kids really look forward to it." Mrs. Kendrick said as she went to help her daughter find some books to take home.

After Laura and her mother left with their bundle of books, Brigid returned to her work. However, it wasn't long before the store became too busy with the late afternoon rush. Soon they were working the register and helping other customers. By five o'clock the crowd dwindled in number. The quiet gave Brigid the opportunity to divert her attention back to the mystery woman. She didn't know why she was so interested in her, but her presence pulled at Brigid's heartstrings. Maybe it was the lost look on her face or the sense of loneliness that bled from her.

Brigid returned to the stacks, nonetheless she spent most of her time thinking about the woman outside. But the evening rush of customers again drew her away and kept her busy, however not too busy to take the occasional peek out the window in hopes of seeing her.

At seven o'clock Brigid found Melissa ringing up a sale at the register. Stan, who helped cover the evening shifts, had arrived an hour ago. Brigid felt more comfortable having him around at night, though the crime rate didn't reach even a medium level in the town. He was in his early thirties and was slightly over six foot five inches tall. He went to the gym enough times a week to look impressive and intimidating, though, neither matched his teddy bear personality.

"Hey, Melissa, I'm going to get going for the night. Stan is in the back helping a customer. You two should be okay to close, right?"

"Yeah, we'll be fine. Have a good night." Melissa wiggled her fingers in Brigid's direction as she continued to help her customer.

Brigid went down the alleyway behind the store to retrieve her car. As she approached the car, she noticed a piece of paper sticking out from under the windshield wiper. Thinking it was an advertisement Brigid pulled the paper off the windshield and read it.

"HI!" The writing was shaky and looked like it was written in the unsure hand of a child.

Brigid smiled, thinking it must be from one of the children who frequented the store. Seeing no one about, she opened the door and got in, and placed the note in her glove compartment.

In the shadows, unseen by Brigid, eyes overwhelmed in fascination watched. Unblinking, the person yearned to reach out and take what they desired and hoped that someday they would have the ability to.

Ellen Hoil

Chapter Three

OVER THE COURSE OF the next few days, Brigid found more notes on her car. The second and third one said "Hello," but the fourth one said "Thank you." She began to think it wasn't one of the children even though the handwriting was in the same childlike scrawl. They were too persistent. Since the notes sounded harmless Brigid decided to accept them in the friendly manner she felt they appeared.

To take her mind off the notes, Brigid continued to mull over the other mystery in her life—the walking woman. Each time Brigid watched the woman eat the sandwiches and other items she left, a sense of warmth settled in her soul. She put her hand over her beating heart and realized it was the first time in a long while she even noticed its existence.

Brigid wondered if the woman and the notes were connected. The timeframe fit. When she gave it more thought, however, her doubt grew. She couldn't imagine someone who read so much leaving such childlike notes.

The scribble didn't fit the image Brigid had of the blonde. Based on the titles she had seen the woman reading when she sat next to her at lunch, the woman was obviously educated. Well educated, at least when it came to reading.

Thursday morning brought a heavy rain that continued into the afternoon. The rain didn't stop the woman from her walk, even though it soaked both her and her book. Brigid watched as she struggled to turn the saturated pages without ripping them. She stopped walking each time to turn a page.

Brigid saw her stand in front of The Wordsmith as she carefully turned a page before she continued her walk. Brigid couldn't bear the sight of the bedraggled woman and her book any longer. She grabbed an umbrella from a box under the counter and left the store. Brigid approached the woman and blocked her way.

"Hi," Brigid said.

Although she hoped for an answer, she didn't expect one. The woman didn't look up from her book but also made no move to go around her. She was trembling. Brigid couldn't tell if it was from the cold rain, or some emotional reaction.

"Remember me? I was wondering if you'd like to come in and warm up for a bit. You're soaked. I can get you some hot coffee, or chocolate, if you prefer."

Lifting her head just slightly, the woman glanced toward the store. Her eyes returned to look down at her feet a second later. Still she said nothing.

"Well, if I can't convince you to step in out of the rain, then at least take this," Brigid said with a bit of harshness in her voice and thrust the umbrella at the woman. "Don't worry about giving it back. I pulled it from the lost and found." The woman reached out and took the umbrella from Brigid. Their fingers touched for the briefest moment. The woman's fingers were cold, but they left a sense of warmth, as if the woman was trying to gather heat from her.

Brigid also felt a warmth somewhere inside herself. But it wasn't a physical warmth. Rather it was an emotional one. The type you felt when surrounded by family or close friends. Brigid was at a loss to explain what she was sensing, or why.

"Please, try and get dry," Brigid said as she stepped out of the woman's way.

The woman stood still another moment before walking away. When next the woman walked by the store, Brigid was relieved to see her carrying the open umbrella in one hand and her book in the other.

Chapter Four

AS THE END OF SPRING came and the summer heat began, the woman allowed Brigid to sit with her as they ate. Brigid could feel the trust between them grow. With that growth, her concern for the woman also grew. Brigid often wondered where the woman went at night. There weren't many streetlights on The North Fork. Only the occasional glow from homes and stores illuminated the road. Once in a while, a passing car's headlights offered a temporary reprieve from the darkness. On the nights she worked past dark, Brigid noticed that the woman vanished as the sun set. She hoped the woman found some rest, some respite from whatever it was she was going to, or from.

One evening late in June, Brigid packed up her briefcase, ready to call it a night. The paperwork and bookkeeping felt like an endless quagmire filling her briefcase to the brim. Clearing the last vestiges of paper off her desk she walked out of her office and into the front of the store. *Wow, it's pretty crowded, even for a weekend. I'll make sure the kids can handle everything without me.*

Naomi, a local flutist Brigid hired on occasion, was playing a quiet classical tune. Her nimble fingers ran up and down the pipe as a soft melody flowed through the store.

"Hi, Brigid," Anthony said when Brigid stopped beside him. He was a Friday night regular. "Naomi sure does weave her mood in her music when she plays."

"You're right. I'm always amazed at how the music fits however she feels that day." As Brigid walked to the register she waved at Naomi. Naomi winked and nodded her flute at her.

"Hi, Stan," Brigid said, noting the growing crowd. "How are things going up here tonight?"

"Pretty busy. Melissa is helping Brendon find a copy of Poe's short stories for his term paper."

"Everyone should own a Poe." Brigid smiled. "Even Brendon Johnsenberg."

Stan laughed. He was a gentle soul, and one of her favorite

workers. He was an indispensable part to her operations, a close second to Melissa. He had worked for Brigid since his senior year in high school and was gentleman enough to walk with the rest of the staff to their cars to make sure they were safe.

"Who's working with you tonight, Stan?"

"Melissa is working until six-thirty and Connie and Denise are working till closing."

"Okay, I'm heading out now myself. I'll just say bye to Melissa. Is she still in the Classics section?"

Stan saw Melissa across the store and pointed to the fiction section where the new books were.

"There she is."

"I'll see you later." Brigid looked at the small crowd that waited at the register. "Why don't you get Connie up here to help you and Denise out for a while?"

"Sounds like a plan. I'll see you Monday."

"Oh, by the way, when do you hear about your final grades?"

"Should be Thursday at the latest. I'm worried about the math, though."

"I'm sure you did fine. Didn't Mindy tutor you?"

"Yeah, she did." Stan blushed and a small smile formed.

"Well, then, I am sure you've got nothing to worry about." Brigid reassured him with a smile.

"Thanks, Brigid."

As Brigid turned to go, out of the corner of her eye she saw a blonde figure walk by outside the store. She stopped to watch before going to look for Melissa. She found her in the biography section, helping a customer get a book off one of the high shelves.

"Hi, Melissa. I'm leaving and wanted to say good night."

"Okay. I'll see you on Monday." Melissa looked down from her perch on the library ladder.

"But you don't work Mondays."

"Yeah, but you forget, I'm working Saturday and Sunday this week. You gave me Friday and Saturday off next week so that Rita and I can go up to Connecticut Thursday night."

"Oh, that's right. I don't know where my mind went for a moment. Sounds nice. I hope you have a good time." Brigid nodded.

"I'm sure it was preoccupied with a certain blonde. Well, if nothing else, I should come back nice and relaxed."

"I left the money on my desk to cover for the weekend."

"You buy her lunch every day, even your days off. It is possible that the woman can take care of herself," Melissa said.

"I'm not so sure about that. Besides, it would make me feel better. Otherwise, I'll end up worrying about it the whole time."

"Okay. No problem. Anything in particular I should get this time around?" Melissa grinned.

Brigid knew she was being made fun of. They went through the same routine every time, but she didn't mind. "Yeah. I think she's into the roast beef and provolone. And make sure you get mayonnaise on it. Oh, and don't forget the lettuce and tomato, and put it on a roll, not bread."

"Anything else?"

"Yeah. Sunday you can get her the meatloaf special. I'd like to know she ate a good balanced meal at least once this weekend, something hot."

Melissa's tone changed. "Okay, Brigid. No problem. I'll take care of it for you. Don't worry about a thing. I know this is important to you. Sometimes I worry about her myself."

"Well, I guess that's everything. If I think of anything else, I'll call you." Brigid looked through her purse for her keys. "I'll see you Monday. If you need me, I'll have my cell phone. Have a nice night."

"I will. Night."

Brigid waved at Stan and Naomi as she left the store. When she reached the parking lot, she saw it. Flapping in the cool breeze was a piece of paper under her windshield wiper. She was a bit surprised. It had been a while since the last note. When she opened the paper, she was startled to find it was not the typical note. Although it was in the same handwriting, it was more than the usual "Hi." Much, much more. As she read the note her watery eyes began to blur the words:

"From childhood's hour I have not been
As others were; I have not seen
As others saw; I could not bring
My passions from a common spring.
From the same source I have not taken
My sorrow; I could not awaken
My heart to joy at the same tone;
And all I loved, I loved alone."

Overcome with a profound sense of sadness, Brigid's body

trembled as she refolded the paper. It was by Edgar Allan Poe. A poet whose melancholy she often identified with. She wondered at the soul that left the note. By now she suspected who had been leaving the notes, and she felt sorrow deep inside herself. She could fathom a life without true, deep abiding love. It was how she herself felt sometimes. But Brigid at least knew she had people who loved her, who would always be there for her and support her. This stranger seemed to have no one. For that Brigid felt a tear begin to fall.

"But why is she reaching out to me? I don't know her. I don't know anything about her, and she doesn't really know me, except for the little I've talked to her.

Chapter Five

BRIGID SPENT THE FIRST part of her weekend as planned. Saturday brought clear skies and warm sunshine along with the aroma of the hyacinth that bordered the woods in her back yard. She got halfway through her book and took long, relaxing naps in the hammock in the early summer sun.

When her dog, Artemis, came around, Brigid would toss her ball. Artemis had adopted Brigid about a year and a half ago when they found each other in the same alley. On occasion, Brigid took Artemis to work for a day of fun. The customers fawned over her, especially the children.

All day Brigid thought about the note left on her car the day before. The title "Alone." She wondered about what the stranger meant to convey by leaving it for her. *I get the feeling that is exactly how this person feels. They're reaching out to me. That is what it is, right? But, what do they want?* Brigid found it hard to connect those thoughts. For the moment, Brigid was content to think that it was one lonely soul yearning for someone to share their thoughts with.

She admitted that she was occasionally lonely. For the most part, Brigid was busy with the store, her friends, and on the weekends and holidays, her family. She had come to be okay with being alone. But at night, when it was just her and Artemis it was harder to not feel lonely. Artemis came back with the ball for another throw. "It hasn't been the same for a while, has it, girl? I bet you miss a bit of company too, huh girl?" Brigid threw the damp tennis ball and grinned watching Artemis chase after it. Their life had been that way for a while now, ever since that one life-changing day.

Artemis came back and dropped the ball at her feet. She gave it a nudge toward Brigid, making her smile. "You're all the company I need. It suits us just fine, right?" Brigid wasn't sure if she felt as convincing as she sounded. "It might be nice to come home to someone who wasn't so furry. Someone who meant more to me." She looked up and the stars reminded her how small life really was in the universe. "We have to treasure life. No matter what is happening around us, Artemis. We will hold it dear. You and me 'til the end." She knew she was talking more to herself at this point.

She noticed dusk brought cooler air. "Come on, Artemis. Time to head in." Brigid held the door as her furry companion moved into the house. As she turned to close the sliding glass door behind her, Brigid looked out at the fields beyond her yard, taking a moment to admire the hues of the sky as the sun set over the treetops. The coolness of the evening air made her shiver. She crossed her arms hugging herself tight to ward off the sense of cold. An instant of remembrance brought a deep sigh from well within her. Brigid looked out the window one last time before she turned and walked away.

***

"Aunt Brigid!" Tyler ran up and hugged her leg. Deidra, his twin sister was not far behind.

"Hi, Tyler. How's my best buddy today?" Brigid bent down and kissed his auburn head and did the same for Deidra.

"I'm okay. Deidra and me got to level three at swimming,"

"That's great. I'm so proud of you." Bridget laughed when the two of them came within reach of Artemis' licking tongue. The twins giggled and tried to fend her off, but failed, making them all hoot harder.

"Mom and Dad took us to Friendly's to celebrate," Tyler said as Brigid bounced him up into the air, caught him, and let him down gently. Each child took hold of one of her hands while they walked into the backyard.

"Aunt Brigid, we made it to level three!" Deidra said, her excitement showing in her large grin.

Tyler rolled his eyes. "I already told her, Deidra."

Laughing, Brigid hugged Deidra. "That's okay, Deidra. I'm still happy to hear about it, and I'm very proud of you both. Where are Mom and Dad?"

"Mom's out by the shed getting our stuff ready for the beach," Deidra said. "Dad's inside working on sandwiches."

"Is Dad coming with us?" Brigid asked.

"Yeah, he's going to let us jump off the rubber dinghy." Tyler walked backwards in front of Brigid.

Brigid saw her sister loading the kids' wagon with all the beach paraphernalia. Based on the large pile of toys, it was going to take a while to get it loaded up.

"Hi, Janet," Brigid said.

"Hi, Brigid." Janet grinned at her sister. "I should be ready in a bit."

"How about I take the kids down now?"

"Okay, I'll be down in a little while."

Bridget turned back to the twins. "All right, kids, grab your bikes and let's get going."

Brigid followed behind the children as they rode their bikes. When they arrived at the beach, the kids parked them next to the stairs down to the beach. The beach wasn't crowded, and it was easy to find the perfect spot. The kids threw their towels to the sand and ran into the waves. Brigid joined them and splashed the kids with the warm salty water.

They played until Janet and David arrived and Brigid made her way out of the water to help Janet set things up. The kids got their toys while David put the inflated boat in the water. Janet and Brigid sat in the beach chairs to watch the kids and David play.

Janet laughed. "Nice to see someone else keep them entertained. So, how are things at the store?"

"Things are going well. Now that summer is here business is picking up. I was thinking of adding a part-time person on the weekends. We have been pretty busy with the weekenders and day-trippers this year." Brigid looked at her sister. "How are things going here? I've already heard the kids' big news."

"The kids have been pretty good lately. I'm amazed though that they haven't hugged the new guinea pigs to death. Why I thought they needed a pet, I'll never know." Janet laughed and shrugged her shoulders. "Other than that, things have been okay. Work at the hospital is going well too. My life is boring."

They sat in silence a moment and watched the kids and Dave play.

"Anything new going on socially?" Janet raised an eyebrow.

"No, Janet, and no I am not looking," Brigid said in a curt tone.

"Okay. I'm sorry if it makes you feel defensive."

"I know you meant nothing by it. This all just gets tiring after a while to have to defend my choices. You know me. I haven't really thought about dating for some time now. I think the last one was about a year ago."

"Oh. Yeah. I remember. It was the disastrous blind date Melissa set you up on."

Brigid cringed at the memory of it. "Who knew someone could

spend three hours talking about their dog on a first date. I've dated before that." Brigid crossed her arms.

Janet narrowed her eyes. "Brigid, you haven't been with the same woman more than two or three times in the last few years. It took you two years to even go out on a date."

"I'm just not that interested, Janet. I satisfied with my life how it is. I don't need anyone else. My heart just isn't into it."

Unbidden, the memories of that day came back.

She hadn't been able to reach Tina all day and that was very unusual. Then the phone rang. The call that brought her world crashing down.

"Hello. Is this Brigid Fitzpatrick?"

"Yes. May I ask who's calling?"

"Hi, Ms. Fitzpatrick. My name is Sergeant Don Simpson. I'm at the Riverview Hospital Emergency Room. Are you the emergency contact for Tina Ballard?"

Somewhere in her mind Brigid took note that his voice was soft and gentle. But at the mention of Tina, a cold fist gripped her heart. She knew. He didn't need to say the words. She didn't want him to. That would make it real. She didn't want it to be.

"Ms. Fitzpatrick, are you still there? I need to know if you can come down to the hospital? There's been an accident."

Four words, and Brigid knew her perfect life was over. Her dreams of growing old with the love of her life was ended.

She slid to the floor and rested against the wall. The phone slipped from her fingers. She let out a gasping sob and tried to cover her mouth to keep the rest in. If she didn't let the pain out, it couldn't be real. Brigid heard the voice coming over the phone.

"Ms. Fitzpatrick, Ms. Fitzpatrick?

She blindly reached for it and picked up the phone, placing it to her ear. Her voice struggled. "Yes. I'm here." She stood up but kept a hand on the wall.

"Can you come to the hospital? Do you have someone who can come with you?"

"My sister. I can call her. Yeah, I can do that. Let me do that." Her mind was going numb. "I have to go now." Before the Detective had a chance to respond, Brigid disconnected the call and stood. She touched her lips, as if she could remember the feel of Tina's lips on hers.

Brigid took her purse off the table by the door and made her way to the car in the driveway. She felt like she was in a fog. She didn't recall starting the car, but the radio came on automatically. The local news anchor was on. She barely paid attention, until she heard the words, "The Expressway is closed at Exit 70 in Manorville due to an accident. Fire and police are on scene."

Without thought she turned the volume up and listened.

"A police investigation is underway after an accident involving a car and a tractor trailer. One person was transported to Riverview hospital in critical condition."

Brigid knew the code phrase, "police investigation." Another way of saying someone was dead or not expected to live.

As tears ran down her face, and she wiped at her nose with her sleeve, she pushed the buttons on her phone, and then heard Janet's voice.

"Hey Brigid. What's up?"

Brigid must have made a sound, since she heard Janet say, "Honey, are you okay. What's the matter?" There was a tone of alarm in her voice.

"Tina's dead." Having said it out loud, Brigid dropped the phone. She began sobbing uncontrollably. Unaware of anything, until Janet was suddenly wrapping her in her arms.

For twelve years Tina had been her life. Twelve years when it ended in a fiery blaze. Brigid still had nightmares thinking about Tina's last moments, alone in the car. The thoughts were too horrifying for her. She would wake up in a cold sweat and sleep eluded her for the rest of the night.

She abhorred the loss of their future together. She knew deep in her heart that there was no one able to replace Tina. They had planned to grow old together. But over the last three years, Brigid resigned herself to growing old alone.

The first year after losing Tina was hard. But as time went on, Brigid learned to be satisfied with work and her family. She was intent on being the best aunt, sister, and friend she could be. Nothing more, nothing less.

"Actually, I did meet someone interesting a few weeks ago. She fascinates me," Brigid said.

"Oh, really?" Janet sat up and leaned forward grinning.

"Don't get any dating ideas. It was nothing like that, Janet. She is a woman I've run into in town. We've been sharing lunch for a while, if you can even call it that." Brigid hoped that her answer would deflate Janet's excitement. Even though a bit of exhilaration swept over Brigid at the thought of the mystifying woman, there was nothing to tell.

"Oh, okay. Is she from around here?"

"I don't know," Brigid said.

"What does she do?"

"I don't know."

"What's her name?"

I know she's just curious because she cares about me. But how do I explain that my thoughts are wrapped around someone I know nothing about. It sounds so lame in my head, let alone out loud. "I don't know."

"Well, what do you talk about?" Janet asked.

"Nothing, really. I go to the deli and buy her lunch, then we either sit on the bench outside or she eats on the go." Brigid hoped her answer would satisfy Janet's curiosity.

"What does she say to you while you're there?" Janet threw her hands up. Her frustration at the answers was evident to Brigid

"Nothing. She doesn't say anything. She just sits there." Brigid grimaced.

Janet grinned. "Let me see if I have this right. You met a woman on the street. You don't know who she is, where she is from, what she does, and you have never talked to her, but you buy her lunch. Is that right?"

"Yes, and I do talk to her on occasion, Ms. Smarty-pants. Only she doesn't talk back."

"Is she at least cute?"

"Gorgeous," Brigid answered with a thoughtful look in her eye.

"Good, I'm glad," Janet said, leaning back in her chair.

"She has been hanging around town for a while. I started to give her something to eat every day because I was a little worried about her. God, Janet, if you could see her. She looks so lost sometimes. I want to go up to her and give her a hug and tell her that everything is going to be okay. I don't know what else to do for her, so I figured the least I can do is make sure she is fed. I felt so bad the other day."

"Why?"

"It sounds stupid I know, but I got busy in the store and didn't get a chance to go to the deli. I could see her stop at the window a couple of times and look in. But it took me a few hours to break away. I felt so guilty almost. Why does she wander around? I want to be able to find out her story, not because I'm curious, but because I have this desire to help her through whatever it is.

"Okay, I won't push. Just be careful. I don't want to see you hurt," Janet said.

Brigid spent the rest of the day with her family, the weather and the company allowed her to enjoy herself. She allowed the stress of the notes, and her concern for the woman to lessen. She felt serene for the first time in a while.

She had fun playing with the kids at the beach, and later they had a water fight with the hose as they rinsed the sand off. David grilled steaks for dinner while Janet made the vegetables and salad. After dinner, Janet and Brigid sat down at the picnic table to talk some more.

"I wanted to get your opinion on something. I found this on my car the other day. What do you think about this?" Brigid pulled the folded note out of her purse and handed it to her sister.

Janet read the note several times before looking up at Brigid.

"Do you know who left it?"

"I have no idea. I've been getting notes on my car for a while now, but this is the first one that said anything other than 'Hi' or 'Thank You.'" She was quiet for a long moment. "I don't know what to make of it. The writer sounds so lonely...so desperately sad for something."

"Yeah, I kind of get that feeling too. I definitely feel the loneliness." Janet paused. "But why send it to you? Do you have any idea who it might be?" She handed the note back.

"I don't know for sure. At first, I thought it was one of the kids, but now I don't think so. I can't imagine any of them doing this." Brigid shifted from one foot to another. A sign to Janet that she was troubled.

"Has anyone been bothering you, or hanging around more than usual?"

"No, there hasn't been anyone new that I've noticed, other than the woman I mentioned. No one acting strange or anything like that. For some reason, I feel a strange connection to whoever wrote it though. I feel like the person picked Poe for a reason. It's as if they identify with him."

"Well, I don't know what to make of it, but be careful, Brigid. You don't know anything about this person. I've seen too much in the ER not to be a little worried about it. I hope you'll keep that in mind."

"I know, Janet. Don't worry. I think this person only wants someone to talk to."

Later that night, Brigid pulled into her driveway with Artemis asleep in the passenger seat. The kids had done a good job tiring out the rambunctious dog. She walked up the steps to the front door, and noticed a piece of paper jammed between the door and the sill. Brigid pulled the paper out as she stepped into the house with Artemis in tow.

> Wealth I ask not, hope, nor love,
> Nor a friend to know me.
> All I ask, the heaven above
> And the road below me.
> AND YOU.

Again, Brigid recognized the words. It was from a poem entitled "The Vagabond," by Robert Louis Stevenson. However, the last two words were not part of the original poem. Now Brigid was worried. It seemed that the person saw her as a form of salvation.

Trying to regain her senses, Brigid went into the kitchen to start the electric kettle for tea. Brigid re-read the note, searching for some clue as to its meaning.

What does he mean, 'AND YOU?' He doesn't even know me, at least not that I know of. Does he think I'm his answer, that I'm the home he's looking for? Maybe Janet is right. Maybe I should be worried about this. I mean, God, he left this at my home. He knows where I live. Did he know I wouldn't be home tonight? Or did he expect me to be here?

Brigid jumped when the kettle went off. "I think we need to do something about this, Artie," she said looking down at the dog.

Brigid made her tea, still anxious about the note. She decided to go to bed and worry about it tomorrow in the light of day. She usually jumped right into bed, but tonight she checked to make sure the house was locked up, even the windows, which was something she never did. Once she was sure that all was protected, she went upstairs to bed with Artemis. She felt more shielded with the dog.

Chapter Six

THE NEXT MORNING, BRIGID opened the shop at nine o'clock, as usual, with her battered briefcase and a cup of coffee from Steve's balanced in one hand, while she held the keys to the store in the other. Most of the time, she didn't mind opening the store alone. It was quiet and gave her time to think about what needed to be done and to catch up on paperwork.

As she undid the lock, and pushed the door open, a small piece of paper fell from the doorjamb. Brigid was caught off guard when she saw it. This was the second change in routine for the note writer in two days. She put her stuff down on the counter, and then retrieved the note from where it had fallen.

> A place in thy memory, Dearest!
> Is all that I claim:
> To pause and look back when thou hearest
> The sound of my name.

Brigid didn't recognize this poem this time. *Did they write it themselves?*

"I don't think so," she said to herself.

The note saddened her. For someone to feel so insignificant in life that their greatest hope was someone would remember they existed broke Brigid's heart. She put the note in her pocket so she would remember it every time she touched it. Though it wouldn't help the writer, it would bring a sense of connection to Brigid as though she was somehow fulfilling her part.

As she leaned against the waist-high counter and drank her tea, the bell on the door rang. Brigid's cup stopped halfway to her mouth. Standing inside the doorway was the blonde stranger.

The blonde looked a little more put together in her blue jeans, faded red polo shirt, and sneakers. Her appearance no longer disheveled. She still needed a haircut. Her hair was shaggy, hanging close to the bottom of her ears and the back of her neck, and the bangs fell over her eyes. The woman stood still for a moment, scrutinizing the wooden floor of the store. Light through the front windows reflected around her.

As if preparing for battle, the blonde squared her shoulders and walked to the far wall. She began to study the titles in the literature section, in the bookcases lining the outer walls of the store. Brigid stared for a moment as she took in the woman. She was surprised she never looked around to take in what was around her.

She perused each book from left to right on the shelf and then moving down to the next shelf. When she got to the bottom of the bookcase, she moved to the next set. From what Brigid could see, the stranger never looked around the store—she never looked away from the books. It was as if the world outside the bound covers didn't exist.

Brigid watched for several minutes as the woman performed her browsing ritual. She could see the woman's brow furrowed in seeming concentration. Her hands clenched and unclenched in the pockets of her pants. Brigid took it as a sign of how nervous she must feel. Brigid understood that the woman didn't want to make conversation. She left her alone as she pulled down books for special orders.

Brigid had been at it for well over two hours when she moved to the pet section to pull a training book for one of her customers. As she came around the corner, she saw her stranger crouched down on the floor reading the titles on the bottom shelf. Brigid stood back and watched how intently she studied the books. Every couple of books she would pull one out and then put it back. She stood up and moved to the next shelf. Brigid noticed she had a pen in between her fingers, tapping it against her leg. She had long, tapered fingers, the kind Brigid's grandmother called pianist's fingers. The woman had several small books under one arm and two larger books on the floor at her feet. She was looking at the back of a book Brigid recognized being about caring for a cat.

Should I, or shouldn't I? Well, it's always said, nothing lost, nothing gained. "Hi, I'm Brigid Fitzpatrick. Can I help you find something?"

The blonde jumped, throwing the pen behind her. Both of the women watched as the pen flew over the stacks. Brigid watched the blonde's profile, hoping for a reaction to her introduction.

The woman also turned back and, for what seemed a long moment, they stared into each other's eyes. Brigid felt herself fall into the bluest eyes she had ever seen. Along with warmth and depth, there was also unmistakable fear. The emotions were gone so fast that Brigid wasn't sure she'd seen them. It was as if a wall had appeared between them.

What I see before me is what Shakespeare called a "soul bruised with adversity."

The woman looked away and back to the book in her hand. Brigid once again realized how beautiful the woman was. Her willowy figure, high cheekbones, strong jaw, and straight nose made her a classic beauty.

"I'm sorry," Brigid said as she reached out to touch the woman's forearm but pulled back before she did. "I didn't mean to startle you. I thought that you might want help finding something in particular."

Brigid knew the real truth was that she felt the need to reach out to this stranger, to maybe give her some connection to something. To Brigid she appeared like someone lost to the present time and place. Her manner was of someone unaware of her surroundings. Brigid wanted her to feel connected. To the store or herself, she wasn't sure.

"It's okay," the woman said after a moment. Close to a murmur, her voice was soft, and rich. The woman made no attempt at eye contact. She continued to look at the cover of the book she held.

"Do you have a cat?" Brigid asked, trying to engage the woman in conversation.

"No," the woman answered in a whisper after first clenching her jaw.

"Okay. Are you getting a cat?"

"No," the blonde said.

Brigid smiled as she tried to reassure her.

"Are you thinking of getting a cat? Maybe I can help you find the right book."

"No!" the woman answered. She began to tremble. She looked ready to jump out of her skin. The woman's one free hand was clenched by her side.

The woman looked at Brigid, her eyes wide, almost like a trapped animal. Brigid stepped aside, unblocking the aisle. The woman rushed past her toward the front of the store. Brigid was afraid if she left, she'd never return. But she stopped just before she reached the door. Brigid watched as the woman took a deep breath, stood up a bit straighter and returned to the shelves and started looking at titles once again.

Brigid got the book she had originally come for and went back to the front counter. She spent the next hour in mindless work labeling and sorting books. When she heard the sound of books being placed on the counter, she turned around. The blonde pushed the pile toward Brigid without looking up. Brigid was a bit shocked. She had expected her to just leave. She certainly didn't think she had the money or wherewithal to come in and purchase anything.

Brigid noticed she had tucked her shirt in and tried to comb her hair a little. She no longer looked as desperate as she had before.

"I'm glad you came in today," Brigid said. "It was nice talking to you. I hope you feel you can drop in anytime...you're safe in here." Brigid had no idea why she said that, but she felt it was important for the woman to hear. Brigid wanted her to believe it.

Brigid pulled the pile of books across the counter. There were seven in all. "Did you find everything you wanted?" she asked, ringing up the first book, the book on cat care. She looked at the other titles. "You have quite a selection here."

The books covered a wide range of unconnected topics. There were books on animals of the arctic, poetry for reading aloud, Tao meditation, a biography on Eleanor Roosevelt, and a fantasy sci-fi novel. There seemed to be no rhyme or reason to her selections. "Well, these should keep you busy for a while." Brigid said scanning the books into the computer.

The woman looked out the front window. Her face was either guilt-stricken or embarrassed, Brigid couldn't tell which. The woman's face flushed. Brigid attempted to put the woman's mind at ease.

"It's nice to see someone enjoy books so much. I know I get lost in my own world when I read. Hours can pass before I notice." Brigid checked the total. "That will be sixty-two dollars and eighty-five cents." She was surprised when the woman reached in her pocket and pulled out a crumpled ball of bills.

She gave Brigid three wrinkled twenties and a balled up five-dollar bill. Brigid didn't want to embarrass the woman any further so didn't straighten out the money.

"I hope you enjoy them. Come back again anytime; it's usually nice and quiet in the mornings." Brigid said as she handed her the change.

"Samantha, my name is Samantha," the woman said in a voice so low and small, Brigid almost didn't hear it. She looked Brigid in the eye before she turned and walked out of the store, leaving Brigid staring after her in shock.

Brigid realized she had been bestowed a wonderful gift, one which she knew she would treasure. She had been given a brief glimpse into the woman's world, one that was gentle, but of a tumultuous nature, she was certain.

"She is eccentric, I will give her that, but those eyes tell me that she has a kind soul," Brigid said to the empty store. A soul that, though anxious, Brigid felt was worth knowing. She believed the woman was more afraid of people than she was of anything else. Brigid let out a sigh and turned back to her work.

Ellen Hoil

Chapter Seven

AT THREE THAT AFTERNOON, Melissa came to start her shift. She found Brigid behind the counter staring at the pile of books on it. "Hi, Brigid. How was your weekend?"

Brigid jumped and clutched her hand to her chest.

"Oh, Melissa! Do not sneak up on me like that!" She looked up at the clock and was surprised to see it was already three o'clock. She wondered how long she'd been daydreaming.

"Sneak? How did I sneak? There's a bell on the door, for crying out loud."

"Yeah, well, just don't do it again."

"What are you doing? You must be a million miles away to have not heard me come in." Melissa came around the counter and put her purse away.

"Nothing. I'm getting an order together. Why? What does it look like I am doing?" She suddenly felt different with Melissa watching her. *It felt changed. When Samantha had been in the store it was comfortable. Now it feels, I don't know. Uneasy. It is as if the peacefulness had been broken. When Samantha was here, it had somehow felt safe.*

"Geez, paranoid much? It looked like you were so deep in thought when I came in that I'd have to send a search party after you."

Brigid gave a small smile at her friend's teasing. "No, only thinking." She wasn't sure why, but she didn't want to tell Melissa about Samantha. It seemed too private. Samantha kept herself apart from the world, and she had a reason for it. Brigid was determined to respect that, but she was also eager to find a way to get closer to her. Something about the woman made Brigid want to protect her.

I've seen frightened animals who looked less scared than she did. I guess I'll have to go slow to gain her trust. I miss her already. She brought warmth to the store.

Ellen Hoil

Chapter Eight

BRIGID SAT ON THE bottom step of her deck tossing the ball for Artemis and watching the setting sun, her legs were stretched out, ankles crossed. She had changed out of her work slacks and shirt in favor of her favorite faded jeans and an old plaid shirt. The outfit was comforting. She'd bought the jeans years ago from the local thrift shop, and now they were worn in all the right places. The shirt had been Tina's and was one of the few things Brigid held on to. It reminded her of when they went camping.

Brigid imagined she caught the whiff of decaying leaves on the forest floor. She remembered it with love. Every fall they went to Vermont for a week of camping at Diamond Lake State Park. For at least a week after, Brigid would complain about the smell of campfires in her clothes. *I would give anything for that again.* Since Tina died, as soon as the weather started turning cool, she would pull out one of Tina's plaid shirts. Though it wasn't cold out, tonight she felt the need to wear one.

As she thought about Tina, tears came to her eyes. She remembered their last trip up to the lake with both fondness and sadness.

The leaves had started to turn, and the landscape was painted in a rich bounty of colors. The weather was too cold to go swimming, but it was perfect for snuggling close to the fire. Their last night there, they sat by the fire pit with Tina on a log, while Brigid sat on the blanket in front of her. Brigid rested against Tina's legs as she poked the flaming logs. The sparks rose into the night sky to mix with the stars.

"Are you cold?" Tina asked, drawing Brigid back to her chest and wrapped her arms around her.

"With you so close, never. You're my personal little furnace. It's why I love you."

"Oh, so it had nothing to do with my good looks, sparkling personality, and quick wit?"

"No. Those were just added bonuses. That and the great sex."

Brigid winced as Tina's finger poked her in the side. "Hey, no need for violence."

"Violence? I'll show you violence."

Tina turned Brigid's head and the kiss that followed was one of heat and passion. As they pulled apart for air, Brigid looked into Tina's eyes and saw the deep love they shared. The firelight shown in Tina's irises, making the passion Brigid saw appear even more primal. But, mixed in, was tenderness.

The night they spent together was one of the best memories Brigid held onto, one of many. Brigid pulled the collar of the flannel shirt to her nose. She could catch Tina's scent on it, though in her heart she knew it wasn't real. Still, it brought a feeling of safety to her. She missed that.

The dog dropped the tennis ball at Brigid's feet bringing her back to now. Mindlessly, Brigid picked it up and threw it into the woods behind her house, letting it get lost among the scrub pine and oak trees for Artemis to find. Meanwhile, her mind continued to wander.

Although she usually enjoyed her time playing with the gentle dog, her thoughts turned to Samantha. She was still surprised that the strange woman had spoken to her. That it was as personal as her name made her feel special.

"It seemed to take a lot of determination and strength to give up even that small part of herself," Brigid said as Artemis dropped the ball in front of her again. She admired the woman for it. Brigid had so many questions about Samantha. She looked down at Artemis.

"I wonder where she's from. She paid with cash, so she isn't a vagrant. But why does she look like she hasn't eaten a good meal in months? Apparently, it's not from lack of money. Why? I wonder where she's staying. The only place near town is the Bay Cove Motel. I suppose she could be staying outside town...or renting one of beach cottages. It makes no sense that she would travel so far just to walk on Main Street. I hope she's not running from trouble somewhere? I hate to think she is."

"What could make someone so afraid of the outside world? She doesn't seem to be the type to cause trouble. Her eyes are too gentle, and too scared. But then again, they say scared animals can be the most aggressive. The question is, what could she be so afraid of?"

Lost in her thoughts again, Brigid continued to sit and play with Artemis.

Chapter Nine

IN THE WANING LIGHT, the stranger watched the woman and her dog play. The stranger studied her as she threw the ball into the trees. From this distance, the stranger couldn't see her eyes, but knew them to be a rich, chocolate color, with gold flecks around the edges. She was only about five feet, four inches tall, much shorter than the stranger. Her face had an angelic quality—square, with high cheekbones, and a wide, strong jaw. The stranger felt it revealed strength of character. This was a woman who could stand up to the ravages of life. The stranger had seen her courage, had seen her stand up to the unknown without fear. But there was also sadness there.

She is a woman to be worthy of. One who would help make me into the person I want to be. She is perfect. A perfect soul. I know she is the one who could save me from this torment that I am being forced to live in. If only I could make her see that she is the person I need. If I could only be close to her, able to touch her and make a place for her in my life, everything would be fine. My life could return, and the darkness would be gone. The quietness would be restored.

The stranger sat and watched, making plans on how to reach Brigid. The stranger knew it would take courage to get close to her. *Once we are close, how will we make this work? How will Brigid react to me as I am now—the real me? Will she like me? Will she accept me? Why would she? I'm worthless. What will I do if she pushes me away? How can I make a future with Brigid Fitzpatrick? There's got to be a way. How can I do this?*

The stranger watched Brigid throw the ball. It hit a tree and rebounded, landing very near the stranger's hiding spot. She heard her call out to the dog. The stranger wondered if the dog fit the name of the goddess of the hunt. If lucky, the answer was no. Artemis ran over for it, but stopped short when she found the stranger. Not moving the stranger kept in position, kneeling in hopes that the dog would simply take the ball and leave. The dog was large, possibly part German Shepard. A low growl came from the dog, which progressed to threatening barks.

"Nice, doggie. Why don't you walk away, and no one gets hurt," the stranger whispered to the dog in a plea. The stranger pulled a sharp blade from a pocket. "I really don't want to hurt you. Please, just go. I don't want to hurt anyone."

"Artemis, you'd better not be chasing those rabbits again," Brigid called, as she placed a hand on her hip. "If you do catch one, you'd better not bring it to me. Don't think I've forgotten about the doorstep incident."

As the dog and the stranger eyed each other. The dog growled again. Then, as suddenly as she started, she stopped. Artemis cocked her head to the side and looked the stranger in the eye. She walked to the stranger, who held out a hand for the dog to smell. Cautiously, Artemis sniffed the offered hand and moved closer. Pushing her head into the stranger's chest, she knocked the stranger backwards. The stranger kept still until the dog ran back to Brigid.

What happened? The stranger laid on the ground shaking from the encounter. The stranger gathered the flashlight and put the knife back in the pocket and watched as the woman and her dog went into the house. The stranger saw Brigid gently rubbing the dog on the head as they entered the house.

After standing vigil for several hours, the watcher saw the lights in the house began to turn off one by one. As each light went out, the stranger felt the connection to the beautiful woman lessen, causing a loneliness so powerful as to be physically painful. It went deep into the core of the stranger's soul and heart. The stranger's breathing became shallow, but the ache remained.

The stranger could see Brigid through the glass as she locked the back door. Finally, the last downstairs light went off, and a few minutes later the light upstairs came on. The stranger, having watched this routine many times before, knew this to be the light in the woman's bedroom. No longer afraid of being seen, the stranger stood in full view of the house and looked up at the window.

What do you look like when you sleep, Brigid? Do you look as peaceful as a child? What do you dream of? Are they peaceful dreams, dreams of tranquility, love and friendship? Someday I want to know the answer to those questions. If I have my way, it will be soon. I will have you in my life, Brigid Fitzpatrick, someday. Someday you will find me worthy.

The stranger moved into the shadows of the yard. After twenty minutes, the stranger's vigil was over when the bedroom light went out as well. For now, Brigid was tucked away safe in her bed.

The stranger stood outside, under the second-floor window, until the night began to turn into the gray of morning. The stranger felt that the closeness to the woman would somehow keep the darkness inside at bay. The stranger looked up at the window one more time and saw Artemis staring out. The stranger stood still, breath held in suspense, waiting for the dog to give its owner a warning. But the dog simply continued to watch the stranger. The two eyed each other until the stranger gave a slight nod to Artemis, turned and walked away.

Chapter Ten

WITH THE WEEKEND OVER Brigid opened the store as usual, her briefcase in one hand and a cup of tea in the other. The last two days had done a lot to ease her mind and soul. Spending time with her family, and then herself gave her time to relax. She felt a sense of calmness she hadn't felt since Tina.

As she unlocked the door and pulled it open, she noticed an envelope on the floor that had been pushed through the mail slot. After she set her tea on the counter, she picked up the manila envelope. There was no address on it and written on the front, in the handwriting she had become familiar with—although not as shaky as it had been in the past—was another poem.

> Here rests his head upon the lap of Earth
> A youth to Fortune and to Fame unknown.
> Fair Science frown'd not on his humble birth,
> And Melancholy mark'd him for her own.
> Large was his bounty, and his soul sincere,
> Heav'n did a recompense as largely send:
> He gave to Mis'ry all he had, a tear,
> He gain'd from Heav'n, ('twas all he wish'd) a friend.

Brigid put her hand to her chest. The sadness and loneliness of the words...'twas all he wish'd a friend was overwhelming. The poem described a life of utter loneliness and desolation. It was obvious that the writer was seeking her out. The question was whether for friendship or something more sinister.

"What does it all mean?" Brigid thought about who had been leaving the notes. The poems and how they seemed to be reaching out to her scared her now. Each one felt lonelier and colder.

Brigid gasped as she stared at the pile of photos she found inside the envelope. Pictures of Brigid; Brigid with Tyler and Deidra at the beach; Brigid talking to Janet in the backyard; Brigid in her own backyard with Artemis. There were photos of her in almost every activity in her life over the past weekend. She clutched the snapshots, almost crushing them, her hands trembling.

"Oh, my God, what is going on? This person is following me. Geez, what if it's someone dangerous? What am I going to do?" Her heart pounded.

Brigid moved behind the counter to place a barrier between herself and the world. She looked out the window. Seeing no one around, she relaxed a little and took a deep breath.

"I don't remember seeing anybody weird or out of place at the beach. Janet's house is in a private community. I'd think that on a private beach a stranger would've stood out. I'm surprised that Artemis didn't see anyone at home."

On the verge of a full-fledged anxiety attack, she took a deep breath to try and calm herself and think about what it all meant. Brigid jumped with a gasp when the bell over the door sounded. Brigid looked up and saw Samantha standing in the doorway. She was more put together than usual wearing pressed jeans, clean sneakers, and a blue short-sleeved polo shirt. Brigid was surprised to see her, since according to Melissa, Samantha seemed to vanish over the weekend.

There had been no sign of her on the streets over the weekend, though the weather was warm and sunny, perfect for being outside. Samantha never showed to pick up her meal. When she called Melissa last night and heard about it, she began to wonder if Samantha was gone for good.

Brigid wasn't angry for wasting the food and money—she had been worried about Samantha. She had no idea where Samantha could be, no way to track her down or call her. Brigid would never know whether she was okay or not. When she had opened the store, she had looked up and down the street for her. When there was no sign of Samantha, she had become worried. But now she was here, and Brigid felt relieved.

Samantha walked further into the store and stopped in front of the counter. Samantha stood rooted in her spot. Brigid watched as she became increasingly nervous and anxious. She began shifting from foot to foot, clenching and unclenching her hands in her pockets. After a moment, Samantha turned and took a step toward the door.

"Hi, Samantha. I'm glad you stopped in today." Brigid hoped her voice sounded upbeat and didn't give away her anxiety. She wanted to keep the woman in the store. Brigid felt safer with her there. Whether it was because it was Samantha or because it was another person, Brigid didn't know. It didn't matter since her new friend was there and that was what she needed.

Samantha's response was, as usual, to say nothing. She stared at her. Brigid watched as her eyes clouded. After a moment, Samantha walked over and put her clenched hands on the counter. She stood up straight, not leaning against the counter She looked everywhere except at Brigid. Finally, she opened her mouth, as if to say something, then closed it, then opened it again.

"Hi, uhm, are you okay? You look upset."

"Oh." Brigid realized she still held the envelope and pictures. "No, I'm fine." She dropped the photos into the plastic trashcan under the counter. Brigid unlocked and prepped the register, busy work to give her hands and mind something to do. She wanted to forget that someone was following her.

"So, how are you today? I heard through the grapevine that you weren't around yesterday. I missed you."

"Uh, I slept most of the day. I think I was tired," Samantha said as she averted her eyes and put her hands in her pockets. After a few seconds, she took her hands out of her pockets but kept them tight-fisted at her side.

"Well, you look rested. I guess it did you some good." *That's the most I've heard her say yet. Maybe she's a little more comfortable here.*

Samantha's hands weren't shaking or fidgeting. She still seemed tense, but not as much.

"Thank you." Samantha gazed into Brigid's eyes.

The two stared into each other's eyes for what seemed like minutes but was in fact only a moment. Brigid saw again the gentle soul she had seen before, but she also saw a calmness that had not been there. She hoped Samantha had come to terms with whatever demons haunted her. She smiled at her and was amazed when Samantha smiled back. Then, as quickly as it came, the smile was gone, and the look was broken.

"Well, I was just going to look around some, if that's okay with you?"

"Oh, sure, no problem," Brigid answered, distracted by the intense feelings she was experiencing. She watched Samantha walk away into the stacks. *Wow, she sounded almost confident.* She spent the rest of the morning ringing up purchases, straightening books, and dusting shelves. She was constantly aware of Samantha's presence in the shop but did not see her around.

Around one o'clock the store traffic slowed enough to allow Brigid time to think about lunch. She went in search of Samantha and found her in the science fiction section. Brigid stood and watched the blonde for a few minutes as she occasionally removed a book from the shelf and put it in a new spot. Her brow was furrowed in concentration.

"What are you doing, Samantha?" Brigid finally asked.

Samantha flinched but did not panic as she had a few days earlier. "These were out of order. I was simply fixing them. Is that okay?" She sounded unsure as she looked at Brigid.

"Yeah, that's fine." Brigid smiled.

"Thanks. I'm almost done with this section. I already did the literature part," she said, as she looked around the store.

Brigid was surprised since the two sections would normally take one person most of two days to straighten out.

"Thanks for the help. I came to see if you wanted lunch. I'm thinking of getting some pizza. You want some?"

"You don't have to do that. Thanks, though." Samantha turned back to the stack.

Before Samantha could answer, the bell over the door rang. Brigid turned and saw Stan as he came to start his shift. When Brigid turned back to Samantha to ask what kind of pizza the blonde wanted, she saw that Samantha was looking in Stan's direction. Her hands were fidgety again, clenching and unclenching. Brigid wondered if it was all people she acted nervous around.

"I'm not that hungry today. I had a big breakfast. I need to get going now." Samantha stood and made her way to the door before Brigid had a chance to respond. She noticed how Samantha avoided Stan on her way out.

"Wasn't that your mystery woman?" Stan asked when he joined Brigid.

"Samantha...her name is Samantha. She came in to look around." Brigid played down the significance of the event and hoped Stan would accept her brief answer. For some reason Brigid felt the need to keep Samantha's secrets although she wondered about Samantha's discomfort and why she felt the need to lie about being hungry.

"Well, from what I saw, she certainly is beautiful."

"Yes, she is." Even though she didn't know Samantha, Brigid knew the truth applied to the inside as well as the outside of her.

Chapter Eleven

THE NEXT DAY BRIGID walked around the building from the parking lot. She came to a sudden stop when she saw a lone figure lurking in the early morning shadows near the front entrance of the store. The envelope of photos she received the previous day still fresh in her mind, Brigid turned to escape but stopped when she realized it was Samantha. She breathed a sigh of relief and continued toward the door as she pulled her keys from her purse.

"Hi, Samantha. What brings you out so early today?"

Samantha wore a pair of pressed khaki pants with a blue button-down Oxford shirt that accented her eyes. The shirt was in need of ironing but appeared to be an expensive brand. Her hair was disheveled, hanging over her eyes, but Brigid found the look adorable. Samantha possessed the rumpled look of a child who had been out to play.

Brigid had the sudden urge to reach up and brush the blonde strands back from Samantha's eyes. It was a habit she had picked up from living with Tina, whose long brunette hair habitually fell into her face. She stood transfixed for a moment, staring at Samantha. *I haven't had that kind of impulse with anyone since Tina. It feels like a betrayal to her somehow. But it feels as if it is sadder not to be able to do it to Samantha.* Brigid knew, deep down somewhere, that the action would calm her.

Surprising Brigid, Samantha began to talk, and fast. It was as if she was trying to rush all the words out. "Good morning, are you all right? Was it something I did? I don't want you to be scared of me. I wouldn't do anything to harm you. You mean too much to me." Samantha's talking came to an abrupt stop. Brigid saw her look down for a moment, so Brigid almost missed her next statement, "We're friends."

Unsure how to react, Brigid said, "No, I'm fine. You just surprised me, that's all."

"Um, I ran out of books. I thought I'd come and look for some more to read. Um, I hope you don't mind me being here so early, but I didn't have anything else to do. Please. Can I stay?"

Brigid smiled. "No, that's fine. "I hope you haven't been waiting too long." The last thing she wanted was for Samantha to leave. After the sleepless night she had, Samantha's companionship would provide a comfortable blanket of security.

"I thought the ones you bought the other day would tide you over for quite a while. Are you telling me you finished all of those?"

Samantha nodded.

Brigid loved the way the woman devoured the written word. "I'm surprised you read them all. I can't believe you finished them that fast."

"Yeah, I'm sort of a fast reader." Samantha's cheeks flushed to a soft shade of pink. She looked up and met Brigid's eyes for a long moment.

The reaction intrigued Brigid. Brigid was honored that she was given a chance to see into the woman's persona. "I hope this means I'll get the chance to see you around more. I want you to feel comfortable here, Samantha, and I hope you can count me as a friend." Brigid unlocked the doors, relieved to see that no notes or packages had been left for her. "Come on in. I'll get you some coffee."

"Actually, uh, I don't drink coffee. I prefer tea, but thanks anyway," Samantha said more to the floor than to Brigid.

"Really, it's no problem. I drink it myself. Do you want regular or herbal?" Brigid bent her head to catch Sam's eyes.

"Regular, please," Samantha said in a quiet tone, a slight smile on her face. "I don't drink herbal. Black teas are my favorite."

Surprised that Samantha was offering up some information about herself, Brigid quickly responded, "Well, you are in luck, my friend, because I happen to have some very nice British blends." Brigid used the word "friend" so easily when thinking of Samantha. "How about a nice Scottish Breakfast Blend?"

"That would be great. Thanks for going to the trouble."

"Like I said, it's no trouble. It's nice to have someone to share a good cup of tea with. I miss it sometimes." She thought about mornings spent with Tina, overlooking the backyard from the kitchen, drinking their tea together. She didn't understand why Samantha always made her think of Tina. "Anytime you want to stop in and share one, just come over and put the electric kettle on."

"Thanks." Samantha met Brigid's eyes again.

Brigid felt an instant connection to Samantha, as if she had somehow opened a window to Samantha's soul. Brigid finished making the tea and gave Samantha the cup, their fingers touching. A warm tingle radiated up her arm. She released it and felt a sudden emptiness. She didn't dwell on it as they headed over to the front counter. She was afraid to. *Would admitting and accepting this friendship mean betraying Tina?* They drank their tea in companionable silence. Brigid was enjoying their emerging friendship. *But that's all it is* she thought to herself.

"This is very good," Sam said in a quiet tone.

"Thank you. It's one of my favorite blends. I find it a delicious way to start off my day."

"Did you really mean it when you called me your friend, Brigid? I mean after all you hardly know me."

"Of course, I meant it, Samantha. I feel I can consider you a friend."

"Oh, okay, it's not something I'm used to. I would like to be able to have a friend."

"Well, you do," A smile came to Brigid's face before she even had a chance to think, but she hoped it conveyed the warmth she felt for her new friend.

***

Samantha knew they had crossed a line over the last two days, and she reveled in what that meant. For her it meant the possibility of attaining a friendship. Friendship was something Samantha wasn't familiar with. It had been a long time since she had someone to call a friend.

"I don't mean to intrude, but can I ask what scared you this morning?" Samantha asked, "You looked frightened until you recognized me."

"No, that's okay."

"Actually, never mind. It's none of my business. I've gone too far. I overstepped my bounds, I'm sorry," Samantha said in a rush.

Brigid paused. "No, Samantha, it's okay. Really."

"Call me Sam, most people I know call me Samantha. But I'd like you to call me Sam." *One look from her, I feel at peace here. Maybe this is where I need to be to find the quietness I need so badly.*

"All right, Sam." Brigid stopped for a moment and then began. "It's really nothing. I don't even know why I'm telling you this, but I've gotten some notes over the last month or so. They have me a little on edge."

"Do the notes frighten you?" Sam's eyebrows raised.

"Not scared, per se, just a tad disturbed. They started out friendly. At first, I thought it was one of the local kids. The notes were simple—Hi and Thank you."

"What happened to change your mind about them?"

"They've taken on a darker tone over the last week or two," Brigid said, her eyebrows furrowed as she stared into the bottom of her cup.

"How are they darker? Are they talking about hurting anyone or you? I can't imagine someone would do that." Sam glanced down at her hands. They griped the mug tighter, leaving her knuckles white.

"No, nothing like that. As I said, I first got the impression it was one of the local kids. Then I thought it was someone older, because they contained some poetry. The messages were of loneliness but also friendship. They struck me as sad, mostly. The idea that someone felt that way made me want to reach out and give him some support. To let him know that someone does care. You know what I mean?" Brigid looked away. "Thinking about it now, I don't understand what made him change the way he did, but the notes got more serious."

"You are so amazing being concerned about someone like that. What makes you nervous about them now?"

"Well, yesterday, I found a package. It was from whoever is leaving the poems." Brigid said, her voice hushed. Sam could see the tears come to her eyes, but they didn't fall. "I don't want to admit to myself how unnerving the whole experience is getting."

"And you have no idea who it could be?"

"No, but…"

"But what? I want to help."

"I thought about going to the police, but I don't think they can do anything since the notes don't make any threats. I just have to be more alert."

"People say you should be aware of your surroundings." Sam put her hand over Brigid's, gently stroking her thumb along the back of it. "It will be all right. I promise."

"You know it may sound strange, but with you here I feel safer than I have in several years. You're doing a lot to keep me calm simply by being here." Brigid turned her hand over and took hold of Samantha's. She gave a gentle squeeze.

Sam caressed her palm and suddenly realized what her hand was doing, almost of its own volition. She jerked it back and stuffed it into her pocket. A swarm of emotions hit her at once. Her eyes darted back and forth, unable to look at Brigid directly. She searched for something to say but could think of nothing.

Oh, my God, oh, my God, oh my God. What have I done, what have I done? She's going to hate me, I know it. She'll hate me and never let me come back. Then what will I do? I've ruined it, exactly like I ruin everything else, and I was so close.

Brigid smiled at Sam and leaned over the counter as she placed her hand on Sam's arm. "Hey, it is all right. I appreciate the concern. You know, you are the first person I've told about the package. I didn't know what to do. I was going to call Janet, but I didn't want to alarm my sister about it since I think she tends to worry about me too much. It's nice to be able to share this with a friend."

Her friend. She called me her friend again. Could she really mean it? Probably not. She's only being nice. It's the kind of person she is. I know I've messed this up. Maybe I should just leave. Yeah, that's what I should do—just go and not come back. I could go somewhere new, somewhere far away.

Panic permeated her body. The thought of leaving this place, this woman, was too much for Sam, so much that it caused a physical ache in her heart.

Chapter Twelve

"SAM, ARE YOU OKAY? Do you need to lie down?" Brigid asked, letting go of her arm.

A light sheen of sweat appeared on Sam's forehead and upper lip. Brigid raced around the counter and took hold of Sam's shoulder with one hand and then caressed her gently on her back with the other.

"Sam, Sam, are you okay? Why don't you come with me and sit down?"

What am I going to do? I have to get out of here. I have to get out of here. Now, now! But Sam felt something holding her in place. Something kept her from running. She wanted to force it back, make it let go. She grabbed the irritating power that held her where she knew she could no longer be and pushed it away. Sam had destroyed her safe haven and she needed to escape.

Before Brigid could react, Sam grabbed at her shoulders hard enough to bruise them. Sam tried to push her aside, but Brigid held onto her by both shoulders now and refused to let go. Sam dragged Brigid toward the door in her attempt to flee.

"Sam, stop, you're hurting me." When Sam stopped, Brigid looked into her eyes and saw unadulterated fear. Brigid wrapped her arms around the quaking woman. "Sam, it's okay. Everything is going to be okay. You're fine here. You're safe. Nothing is going to happen, and nobody's going to hurt you." She stroked Sam's back, hoping the soothing tone and touch would calm her.

Sam let go of Brigid and hugged her. Sam held on to her like a lifeline. She laid her head on Brigid's shoulder and, for a moment, remained there. *What have I done to deserve this gentle woman's touch? Why does she have such an effect on my mind? She pushes back the racing thoughts and brings me calm. Why can't I deserve this?* Sam's muscles begin to relax but a heart-wrenching sob broke the silence.

"You're breaking my heart, Sam. How can I help you?" Tears soon ran down Brigid's face as Sam felt the grip on her tighten. "The pain you must be in, Sam. What are you fighting? Why do you always feel the need to run?"

"I'm sorry, I'm so sorry. I didn't mean it. I didn't mean it!" Sam said through her tears.

"Why are you doing this to yourself? I told you there is nothing to be sorry about."

Brigid continued to run her hands over Sam's back and then caressed the blonde strands of hair with her fingertips. She leaned back and Sam sensed her grip let go. Freeing one hand, Samantha felt it brushing the hair away from her face.

"So thick and silky. So unlike Tina's hair."

Sam stopped sobbing though she still rested her head on Brigid's shoulder. She nestled her face in the crook of her neck and took several deep breaths. Brigid continued to hold her and rub her back, whispering softly.

"You're fine here, Sam. Nothing is going to happen. Calm down, take deep breaths, you're safe."

Even as she stopped crying, Samantha knew nothing would ever be okay. It never was. *If I could only have someone like you in my life, Brigid Fitzpatrick. Someone who could bring me the rest I need so badly. In your arms I feel safe and protected again, for the first time in so long.*

"I don't deserve you," Sam mumbled. Once Sam felt under control, she stood up and stepped away, immediately feeling the loss of the warmth Brigid provided. She stood, shifting her weight from foot to foot, looking at the floor. "I should go."

"I don't think you should. But if you need to, at least let me take you home. I want to make sure you're okay, and this way we can spend a little more time together."

Sam gave her an uncertain look. "Okay." Sam's shoulders slumped.

"Let me just put up the 'closed' sign and I'll drive you back to your place. Where are you staying?"

"At the Bay Cove Motel, right at the end of town, down by the Mini-Mart."

"I'll take care of you."

As she looked into Brigid's eyes, Sam knew at that moment she could believe Brigid meant it down to her soul. Brigid grabbed her purse from behind the counter and took Sam's hand as she led her to the door.

Sam looked at their joined hands, amazed that Brigid was even willing to touch her.

***

The ride to the motel was quiet. Brigid glanced at Sam, who spent the ride looking out the side window. She seemed to be watching the scenery go by, but Brigid could see the slump of her shoulders. Brigid was still struggling with what happened in the store.

"It certainly turned into a nice day. I hope the rest of the summer goes as well. Are you sure you're all right, Sam? You changed so fast. What happened? One minute you seemed happy and the next you looked like you were having a panic attack." Sam didn't answer her, but Brigid couldn't stand the silence.

"I'm glad you stopped by today. You listening helped me with my problem." Brigid glanced at Sam, who still looked out the window. "You know, I was thinking. It's been nice having you around the store lately, and the work you have done has been helpful. I was wondering if you could come by in the mornings and hang around the store. You could do whatever you feel like, either look around for something to read, or help me out doing stuff. What do you think?"

Sam continued to look out the window for a few more seconds before turning and looking out the front window. "That's okay, Brigid. I know that, after today, you really don't want me there. You're being nice. I understand. You're that type of person. As my father used to say, 'You're one of the good souls.'"

"Sam, one of the things you need to know about me is I rarely say things I don't mean. I really do want you to come back to the store. I truly like your company there, and the free help is nice, too."

"That's mine over there," Sam said when they arrived at the motel, pointing to room eleven. Sam opened the door and began climbing out even before Brigid rolled to a stop.

"So, I'll see you tomorrow? I'll even throw in free pastry from Michloski's," Brigid said before Samantha could shut the door. She smiled, hoping she would see Samantha again rather than lose her. "Come on, Sam. You can't deny me that pleasure."

Sam slowly leaned back into the car, smiling. "Sure, I'll see you tomorrow."

The fears of the day seeming to vanish with every moment. Happy that she gained the promise, Brigid sat and watched as Sam closed the car door and went to her room and disappeared inside. Tomorrow, she already anticipated tomorrow.

Ellen Hoil

Chapter Thirteen

BRIGID WAS DISAPPOINTED WHEN she didn't see Samantha waiting for her the next morning. *I guess yesterday was too much for her to deal with. Maybe I'll stop by later and check up on her now that I know where she's living. I just hope she doesn't think I'm intruding.* When Brigid got to the store door, she saw a slip of paper in the doorjamb. Brigid hoped it was from Sam, but a chill ran up her back when she recognized the handwriting.

> *Doth perfect beauty stand in need of praise at all?*
> *Nay; no more than law, no more than truth,*
> *No more than loving kindness, nor than modesty.*

The tone of the notes had changed again. Gone was the loneliness and despair. In its place was this lyrical piece of poetry. *What a sudden turn. It's too creepy to even consider. Given the photo's I got, I feel almost violated. Who would do this? I might suspect Sam but other than those few recent periods, I know where she is. Plus, where would she pack a camera?* Brigid put the note in her pocket and unlocked the door, checking her surroundings as she did.

Brigid let the matter drop as she began to open the store for the day. The books usually brought her joy, their stories filling the room with companionship. But now, an unexpected solitude fell over the room and left Brigid feeling empty. The warmth and comfort she so often found among the various tomes was lost to her. Brigid didn't know if it was because of the stalker, or Sam's absence.

When everything up front was ready for the day, Brigid went to the back room to bring boxes of new books out to be shelved. As she did the work, her thoughts returned to the notes. The bell over the door rang as Brigid brought the last box out. She looked up to see Sam standing in the doorway. Sunshine poured over Sam as she paused in the entrance, giving her an angelic appearance. *The poem could be about Sam—simple beauty.*

"Hi, Brigid. How are you today?" Sam asked as she approached Brigid.

It took Brigid a moment to notice the difference in Sam. Sam walked toward her with confident strides, and, for the first time, her head was held high and she made direct eye contact. Brigid marveled at the new image, absorbing this new persona.

"Hi, Sam. I was just about to put these books out. I'm glad you came by." Brigid smiled.

"Here, let me take that for you. Where do you want it?" Sam took the box from Brigid.

"Oh, just put it over there," Brigid said, pointing to the section on European travel. "You look really good today. What has you in such a good mood?"

"Nothing special. It's just that I feel really good today. It's a nice day out, and I get to spend time with a good friend." Sam smiled.

Even though Sam was smiling, Brigid could sense something still wasn't quite right. She decided not to ask since Sam was in a good mood.

"Well, I don't know what brought this on, but you look really good. You deserve to be happy."

"Thanks. I woke up and just felt lighter, like I could do anything. I got a good night's rest for a change. Do you want some help with these?" she asked, putting her hand on the box in front of her.

"You don't have to do that, Sam. You could just sit and read if you want to. I can handle this."

"Thanks, but you said I could help out if I wanted to and I want to. I'll admit I have some pent-up energy today, plus this way I get to see the new books first," she said, grinning at Brigid. "Remember, I still need to refill my book supply."

"Why don't you help yourself to some of the tea and pastry I promised, first? I got some fresh jelly donuts." Brigid led her to the coffee center, where she pulled a small pastry box from under the counter. "Here, take one. They are the best in the area."

"Mmmm, my favorite. They look great. Have you been spying on me?"

Brigid stiffened and frowned. For a moment neither of them spoke. Finally, Sam said in a flurry of words, "Oh! Brigid, I'm so sorry. I should never have said that. It was completely insensitive of me. I'm sorry. Please forgive me."

"No, that's okay. I know you meant nothing by it." Brigid saw the desperate look on Sam's face. "It's just that I found another note this morning. It has me on edge, I guess."

"Was it another package?"

"No, it was just a note, like the others. I'm probably overreacting. It was nothing really. It's scary to think of myself as the subject of such attention."

Sam put her hand on Brigid's shoulder and gave it a light squeeze. "Hey, it'll be okay. I bet in no time at all this will be over and a distant memory. You might even find some good came from it."

Brigid almost missed what Sam said, she was focused on the hand resting on her shoulder. She was amazed, and a little confused by Sam's sudden change of temperament. Gone was the unsure timidity, replaced by a deeply caring and consoling person.

"Maybe you're right, Sam. I hope so, although what 'good' can come of this I can't imagine. But it worries me that he's becoming so fixated on me. This last note was so personal."

"Personal? How?"

"Here's the note I found this morning." Brigid pulled the note out of her pocket and handed it to Sam.

Sam read the note aloud and looked up at Brigid with a small grin. "Well, if nothing else, I would have to say I agree. You are beautiful. But I think I can understand how this would make you feel awkward. It seems to be meant on a much more personal level than a secret admirer. Maybe this person is hoping for a deeper connection."

Brigid was shocked. *Did she just say I'm beautiful?* She smiled slightly at the thought. "I guess on some level it is flattering. Wait, what am I saying? A stalker left that note. Not some love-struck kid or lover."

"Are you positive you don't feel too afraid here? I don't think you seem comfortable being alone like this."

"I think it will be fine." Brigid didn't sound so sure. "When the store is open, people come in all the time. I can have Melissa come in earlier in the day and have Stan hang around the nights I close. That should help."

"I would feel better if someone was here with you." Sam looked down for the first time that morning. "You know, I don't do anything most of the day. I could hang out here instead of outside."

Brigid sensed Sam's skittishness returning. "I couldn't ask that much of you, but I appreciate the offer."

"Hey, it's no problem. I can just hang out, read. Maybe I can help you out with a few things if you need me to."

"Okay, if you think it's not too much." Brigid looked into Sam's eyes for any sign of doubt. "Then I would welcome the company."

"Great, I'll start by making some tea. I haven't had my first cup of the day yet, and I'm a bear without it." Sam smiled.

"Oh, I know how that is. Tina was the same way."

"Who's Tina?" Sam asked. Her voice flat.

Brigid noticed Sam's jaw clench but thought little of it. Sam was difficult to read sometimes, as her body language would say one thing while Brigid heard her say another. Brigid's lips drew into a thin line as her deep sadness surfaced.

"Tina was my partner."

"You had a business partner? Did you have a falling out?"

"No, she was my life partner. She died a few years ago in a car accident. It still feels like I lost part of myself when she died...as if a part of my heart was lost. I sometimes wonder where we would be in our lives if it hadn't happened. Would we have kids by now? Would her hair have started going grey at the temples? Things like that. Sometimes I miss her so much."

"I'm sorry," Sam said. "So, I take it you still love her. Why haven't you found someone else to be in your life?"

Brigid looked at Sam puzzled. Sam's tone didn't sound as sympathetic as her words did. *Stop reading into everything she does.* "I've never really looked. Tina and I were college sweethearts and we were together for so many years. I expected to grow old with her. In a way, I think I still do."

Brigid felt a sharp pain in her throat as she remembered— remembered their love, how strong and deep it ran, remembered the phone call, going to the hospital, arranging the funeral. She remembered every moment of their life together and its end as if it was playing in front of her—a slow motion movie of every laugh, teardrop, and embrace. She swallowed the chokehold that pressed against her vocal cords.

"I miss her so much. I've dated some since then, but nothing was ever serious. I don't think it ever will be. I haven't met anyone who can touch my heart the way Tina did. I don't think I will."

Sam stood at the sink with her back still toward Brigid, her head down. "It sounds like Tina was a wonderful person. I'm sorry I didn't get a chance to meet her," she said in a quiet voice.

"I am too. You two probably would have gotten along great."

Sam straightened up and turned toward Brigid. "I am sure we

would have," she said with a smile that didn't reach her eyes. "Well, the kettle is on. Why don't you do the honors while I start opening those boxes for you?"

After Brigid poured the tea, she went in search of Sam. She found her sitting on one of the unopened boxes with her head in her hands and looking as if she'd lost her best friend.

"Hey, you okay?"

"Yeah, I'm fine," Sam said, with a slight smile. "I guess I didn't get as much sleep as I thought. I'll be fine once I get this tea into me."

Brigid didn't push, but she wondered why Sam's eyes were bloodshot and red.

"Here." Brigid handed her a mug of tea.

"Thanks. I'm sure it will help." Sam accepted the cup with both hands and sipped the hot beverage.

"Sam, can I ask you a personal question?" Brigid leaned back against the stacks.

"Sure, what do you want to know?" Sam's eyebrows furrowed.

"How did you come to be here?"

"Here in Riverview, or here in the store?" Sam grinned.

"Both, I guess," Brigid said, shifting her feet. She worried that she might be pushing Sam too far.

"Well, how I got to Riverview is the easier question to answer, I guess." Sam pulled a book off the shelf and looked at its back cover.

"I lived and worked near Springfield, Illinois. I was an attorney there practicing matrimonial law—you know, divorces, child custody, child support...that kind of stuff. I'd been working on a case where a mother wanted custody of her children back and it was my job to make it happen. Personally, I wouldn't let that woman look after a dog. Before we went to trial, I stayed up two nights trying to figure out a way to make her come across as a fit mother. But on the morning of the third day, I decided that I couldn't put up with all the crap anymore. I walked into my partner's office and told him I quit and that he could arrange to buy me out, but I was leaving. I went home, packed up a few things, got in my car, and left.

"I got on the road, and when I had the choice to go east or west, I chose east. I don't know why. I just got a sense that it was the way I needed to go. I felt like I had to be somewhere. It was strange, now that I think about it." Sam looked off in the distance, and then shook her head.

"Anyway, I just started driving. I kept heading east. When I got through New York City I kept going. Following the road more than the signs. I got on I-95, which lead me further east to I-495, and I followed it. By the time dawn came around a day later, I had hit the end. The road ended...I sat until morning on the side of the road thinking how strange it was to actually have driven to the end of such a long road. I finally took the off ramp and ended up on Main Rd. Once the sun was up over the treetops, I saw the sign for the Bay Cove Motel. It was the first place I saw to stop around here, so I did." Samantha returned the book to its position on the shelf and let out a deep sigh. "There isn't much more to it than that, really."

Brigid was amazed. She didn't know how far it was from Springfield to Riverview, but she was pretty sure it wasn't a drive that could be done in a day. Sam made what she did sound so matter of fact.

"Did you stop along the way?"

"No, not really. I stopped for bathroom breaks once in a while and took a nap at one of the rest stops for a few hours, but I wasn't tired or hungry much of the way. When I got to the motel and checked in, I slept for a few hours, but that was about it."

"Why were you out on the streets all that time?" Brigid frowned as she put her hand on Sam's shoulder.

Sam looked at her hand and then at Brigid. "To be honest, I don't know." She gazed into Brigid's eyes. "When I woke up in the motel, I was feeling restless and I couldn't sit still. I felt like I had to be moving. As if I had to be doing something. I tried reading some of the books I brought with me, but I couldn't sit still. Finally, I decided to go for a walk. I grabbed a book and started walking. It helped. I felt better when I was walking. It relieved some of the restlessness. The reading let me get lost too, helped me become invisible. I needed that. I wanted to be nobody for a while. I don't know why, I just did. Once I got here, I came to love things about this town, so I decided to stay."

"Why did you decide to come in here?" Brigid didn't want to push Sam but needed to know.

Sam looked at her, into her eyes and into her soul. "That's a tougher question. I guess because you're here. You're my only friend." Sam stood up and put her empty mug on the top of the book stack. "Come on. Let's get these books out. They won't get themselves on the shelf."

Chapter Fourteen

WHEN MELISSA WALKED INTO the store later that afternoon, she saw Brigid at the front counter ringing up a sale, but what caught her eye was Samantha.

"Brigid, what is she doing in here?" She asked as she went behind the counter.

"Oh, she's helping Mrs. Gabrielson find a book," Brigid said, as she completed a transaction.

When Samantha came to the counter with Mrs. Gabrielson. The elderly woman held two books in her hands.

"Brigid, we decided on *The Art of Pruning* and a science fiction novel." Samantha smiled and turned to her new acquaintance. "You will really like that one, Mrs. Gabrielson."

"Thank you, Samantha. You have been a great help. I never would have picked out that last book, but you made it sound so exciting." Mrs. Gabrielson put her hand on Samantha's arm, and she smiled at her. "Now I can have something to talk to my grandson about. He's very into science fiction and I don't think he's read this one."

"It was my pleasure. Have fun reading them. Maybe you can bring me one of your famous roses one day." Samantha winked.

Samantha turned to Melissa and held out her hand. "Hi, I'm Samantha. It's nice to meet you."

Melissa examined the hand with a bemused look on her face for a moment before clasping it. "Hi, I'm Melissa. Nice to meet you, too."

Samantha turned to Brigid. "I finished emptying the boxes in the back. I thought I would start on the ones in the front now." She jogged off to find another box to empty.

After a moment, Melissa turned to Brigid. "What is going on? And don't say 'nothing'. I'm not buying it," she said, wagging a finger at Brigid. "That woman has been outside for weeks and weeks not making any contact with anyone that we know of. Now she is not only in here but appears to be working here as well. So, what is the deal?"

Brigid looked at her with a smug grin and crossed arms and smiled.

"She has stopped in once or twice in the mornings the last few days. Yesterday she came in and we talked a little bit. Samantha decided she liked it in here, so I'm letting her help out if she wants to."

"Oh, no. There's got to be more to it than that. Someone doesn't just change like that, not without an ulterior motive," Melissa said, pointing a finger at her.

Brigid reached out and pushed it down. "You're partially right. There is a little more to it, but that is basically what happened. I don't know why she's different, but she is. I don't see any ulterior motive, other than her wanting to change. She's a wonderful person and I like her." Brigid smiled, though her smile slowly turned to a frown. "The other reason is because she's sort of keeping an eye on the place."

"Why would you need someone to do that? We don't have a big shoplifting problem here. It's Riverview, for crying out loud. I don't think I even have a key for the front door to my house, let alone do I lock it."

"No, it's more than that. I've been receiving some notes lately. For the most part they've been harmless, but lately they've made me realize someone is following me."

Melissa reacted with a frown and furrowed brow. "What? You should go to the police. How long has this been going on? I bet it involves this Samantha woman."

"No, I already thought of that. I have nothing to show the police since I didn't keep the notes. Besides, like I said, up until now they were harmless. But Samantha was here when I got a package with pictures of me in it. That's when I told her about them, and I thought about going to the police, but I told her I decided I didn't want to do that. She offered to hang out here to keep an eye on me. Why would she do that if she was involved?" Brigid was near tears, the stress of the last few days catching up to her.

"I'm sorry, Brigid. I shouldn't have shot off my mouth. It's up to you how you want to handle this, but I'm worried for you. I would hate to see anything happen," she said as she gave Brigid a quick hug. "It's okay with me if having Samantha here makes you feel safer. Not that you need my permission."

"Thank you for understanding," Brigid said, wiping her eyes.

Melissa looked toward Samantha, who was still emptying boxes. "I must admit she's like a whole new person. A few days ago, I swear if you said 'boo' to her, she would have hit the ceiling."

"Yeah, she does." Brigid smiled. "I think she just worked through whatever was bothering her. Sam is enjoying the new freedom that brings."

Brigid looked over at Sam busying herself with the books. As if she knew they were talking about her, Samantha glanced up and smiled back.

"Hey, Melissa," Sam said. "Would you like to help me clean up the children's section? It's a real mess over there."

Melissa looked at her for a moment as if she was some strange entity.

"Umm, sure, I guess so."

Brigid smiled again.

Melissa gave a sideways glance at Brigid. "Don't be smug. It's unbecoming."

***

Melissa watched Samantha most of the day. Despite what she said to Brigid, something about Samantha made her cautious. Melissa thought it strange that this woman came into The Wordsmith just as Brigid needed someone to lean on. Unlike Brigid, she wasn't so willing to trust this stranger, and when push came to shove that was exactly what Samantha was around here.

As Melissa shelved books, she watched the back of Samantha's head as she sat in one of the chairs reading. She observed as Sam wandered around the store sorting books and, occasionally, helping some customers. She seemed to go out of her way to be helpful, though she didn't seek people out. For an unknown reason, the customers just seemed drawn to her.

"You know staring at me won't make me disappear," a voice said behind her.

"What makes you think I want you to go?" Melissa said when she recovered from being surprised by Sam.

"Because you're Brigid's best friend, and if it was me in your shoes, I'd want me gone as well."

"You're right. I am her best friend and I don't know you from Adam."

"Well, then maybe we should introduce ourselves," Samantha said as she stepped closer and extended her hand. "I'm Samantha."

Melissa looked at the offered hand for a moment and then looked Sam in the eyes. She decided to go along with the re-introduction. "Hi, I'm Melissa, and if you do anything to hurt Brigid, I'm going to have to kill you. Okay, maybe not me personally, but I know people." With that, she shook Sam's hand.

"I'll keep that in mind." Samantha grinned. "Honestly, Melissa, the last thing I want to do is hurt Brigid. She means the world to me. She's offered me something that I never thought I would have...friendship."

"Be careful of that friendship, Samantha. It's not something Brigid gives away easily, at least not since Tina."

"Brigid told me about Tina. I can see how much pain she is still in. I'm honored that she shared her love for Tina with me. She loved Tina very much."

"Yes, she did," Melissa said. "They were each other's world. I thought it would destroy Brigid when Tina died. As it is, I think she only tolerates life now. She goes through the motions, but deep down I know she only does it for the sake of her family and friends."

"I won't do anything to add to her hurt, Melissa. I just want Brigid to be happy. I hope that I can help her achieve that."

Melissa was surprised about how much she had shared and how comfortable it was to talk to Samantha. She decided to give the woman a chance. "What are you reading?"

"A Civil War narrative."

"Oh, I love history, though I've never read that particular author," Melissa said as she looked at the cover. "Isn't this one like three or four volumes?"

"Yeah, three actually. I'm up to the end of the first one."

Melissa was impressed at the size of the book Samantha held. She knew the volume was at least five hundred pages long.

"I haven't decided if I'm going to read the other two or move on to something else yet."

"Well enjoy it. Let me know what you think about it."

Chapter Fifteen

BRIGID LIFTED HER FACE up to soak in the heat from the sun as she left the store at the end of her shift. She enjoyed the warmth on her skin. As she walked down the street thinking about Sam. *I don't know why, but just knowing Sam is so concerned makes me feel safer.*

"What are you doing?" a female voice called in a low tone as she passed the alley next to The Wordsmith.

Brigid jumped and turned around, her hand going on chest. Sam stepped out of the shadows and Brigid sighed with relief. "My shift is over. I'm going home for the day."

"But aren't you going to take your car?" Samantha looked down the alley.

"It's going to be such a nice sunset, so I thought I'd walk home. My sister can pick me up in the morning."

"Oh."

"Why? Is there something you wanted?"

"No." Sam said although she looked unsure.

"Okay, then I guess I'll see you tomorrow," Brigid said as she turned away. Before she could get started, Sam grabbed her arm and held on.

"Sam?" Brigid asked looking down at the hand on her, not sure how she felt, but she looked up into Sam's eyes.

"Uh, I just thought you might like some company on your walk. Do you think it's a good idea to be walking alone considering you got another note today?"

"You're right. The nice weather is so inviting I didn't even think about that."

"I could walk with you, if you would like." Sam shifted on her feet. "I've got nothing else to do, and it'll be too dark for me to stay out here much longer."

"Sure. I always like to have a good companion to walk with me." Brigid smiled. *Her shyness is kind of cute.*

Sam took Brigid's hand.

"Tina and I used to do this all the time. I guess that's why I didn't think it was a big deal. She came to the store to walk me home when her schedule allowed." Brigid sighed. "Sometimes she brought a flower or surprised me with an ice cream cone for the trip home, some small token that made my day. God, I miss her." Tears began to well in her eyes, but she smiled when she felt Sam's fingers squeeze her hand.

***

Brigid's house lay just outside town near the bay. She and Sam walked in comfortable silence, still holding hands.

"What did you do today besides rearranging my shelves? I didn't get a chance to see you as much as I wanted," Brigid said letting go of Sam's hand.

"I hope you don't mind, but some people that came in thought I worked there."

"I don't mind, unless you gave them free books." Brigid chuckled.

"No, no, I would never do that. I wouldn't lie to you."

"I know that, Sam. I was just kidding," Brigid reached and gave Sam's arm a gentle squeeze and let go. "I trust you."

"You do?" Sam asked with a surprised look on her face. "Why? You don't even know me."

"But I think I do."

"How?"

"Well, I saw you with some of those people today. You talked to them and made them feel welcome in the store. You made each person you talked to believe they were special. I saw it in their smiles when they came to pay. That tells me a lot about you."

Sam walked along in silence for a few minutes. "What does it say?"

"I know you are kind, patient, intelligent, and brave, all qualities to be admired in people nowadays." Brigid stopped and looked at Sam.

Sam ducked her head down. "How do you see all that? I don't, especially not brave. Where did you come up with that?"

"I saw it in your actions today. With the children you were patient, taking the time to show them where to look and listen to what they found interesting. When the teenager came in, stressed over her English assignment, you educated her while making the work fun for her. You displayed a good deal of knowledge about the subject she was looking into and took time to talk to her about it. And the way you talked to Mrs. Gabrielson made her feel excited, and I could swear she felt

62

younger at heart."

"It was Walt Whitman." Sam said lifting her head when Brigid continued to look at her and seeing Brigid's confused expression. "The teenager...the report she had to do was on Walt Whitman. I was just trying to be helpful."

"That's it. You were being helpful, ready to lend a hand to someone you didn't know. Did it take a lot of courage for you to talk to her?"

"I was a little scared," Sam admitted.

"A little. I know you well enough now to see you were more than a little scared, but you overcame it and talked to her anyway. You knew things about Whitman's life that made it fascinating and enjoyable for her. That takes real fortitude and intellect."

Sam blushed at the compliment, feeling anxious. "I still don't see it."

"You don't have to. I see it just fine for both of us. I can tell by your actions that you are an outgoing, confident person. You just have to get comfortable around here."

"Maybe," Sam said.

"I'm sure time will prove me right. You're not scared now, are you?"

"No, never around you. You make me feel safe."

"Good, I'm glad."

Brigid took hold of her hand again. The two continued their walk toward Brigid's house.

"Are you chilly? Your hands are cold and shaking."

"A bit." Sam hoped Brigid didn't see the lie reflected in her eyes.

"Well, we're here. Why don't you come in for some tea and warm up a little?"

"No, I should get going. It'll be dark soon." Sam looked toward the front door before looking back at Brigid and extricated her hand.

"You're right. I don't want you out walking in the dark." Brigid looked at the setting sun. "I worry about you, out alone at night." Brigid reached out and Sam felt her hand brush up against her own.

For a moment Sam held her breath. She let it out and looked into Brigid's eyes. "I'll be fine. Go ahead. I'll watch you 'til you get inside."

"You don't think we were followed, do you?" Brigid remembered the reason for her escort. The reality of it took hold again and she looked around.

"No, I'm sure we weren't. I've been keeping an eye on things while we've been walking. I haven't seen or heard anything." She tried to instill a calming, yet confident tone to her voice, as she squared her shoulders.

"Okay. Be careful walking home."

"I will. Don't worry."

"I'll try not to, but this whole thing has me a little bewildered."

"You'll be fine. I promise."

"I believe you, Sam." Brigid looked into Sam's deep blue eyes,

"Good. Now get inside before you get cold."

"Sure thing, Mom," Brigid said, before turning to go.

Sam could feel Brigid watching her as she walked away. Once she reached the street, she glanced back as Brigid entered the house. After she was inside Sam observed the lights going on inside and the outside lights. Sam turned and walk into the darkening night.

Chapter Sixteen

FOR THE NEXT FEW DAYS, Sam spent almost all her time in the store helping with the day-to-day work. She assisted customers in finding books and recommending similar ones. Sam also spent a lot of time reading books she bought. Brigid told Sam she didn't need to pay for them, but Sam insisted so Brigid gave up.

When Sam wasn't working, she was usually in a corner, sitting in one of the comfy armchairs, with her nose in a book. Sam picked books from various sections, almost as if she was unable to decide on a topic of interest. She read travel guides, cookbooks, science fiction, history, and everything in-between. Brigid thought she saw her reading one or two lesbian novels, and it made her insides go warm. Although Sam read almost anything, Brigid wondered about that choice. She knew she wouldn't ask Sam about it, even though she wanted to. Her memories of Tina were too strong to ignore.

Thoughts about Tina and Sam were shelved while she worked the front counter. She tried to push the growing feelings for Sam away. However, they continued to make themselves known. She accepted Tina's death, as much as she could. But lately when she thought of Sam, and her own growing feelings, her soul felt weary. The sense of betrayal was almost too much to bear and she would feel the tears start to fall.

Brigid was excited about the weekend. She planned to spend most of Saturday off to be with her sister and her family. Once Stan arrived for his shift, she planned to take off as soon as she could. She already had her mind focused on her time away. She hoped the time away from Sam could help her put her feelings back where they had started. Brigid didn't want them growing further.

Brigid bought the twins' birthday presents weeks earlier and was energized thinking about their reactions at the small family gathering Janet had planned. Besides her, the twins, Janet, and Dave, Brigid and Janet's mom would be in attendance as well as Dave's parents. It was refreshing how well they all got along together.

Brigid looked around the store, knowing she would miss it even though she was looking forward to her days off, she saw Sam sitting in a chair near the window and was sad she wouldn't see her over the weekend.

Brigid knew Sam wouldn't lack for company since she had made new friends among the regulars, and Melissa and Stan had accepted her. But the thought of being away from Sam that long made Brigid lonely in a way only Tina had before.

"Hey, Brigid. Hey, Melissa. How's it going here?" Sam said. Brigid had been so lost in thought she hadn't seen her walk up.

"Hey, Sam. Things have slowed down a little." Brigid realized she was admiring the beautiful woman. The shaggy blonde hair was hanging over her eyes. Brigid felt the urge to run her fingers through them.

"Great. Can I lend a hand up here later if you need it?" Sam asked. "I promise not to play with the paper for wrapping books again, even though I just read this neat book on Origami. I could make you a nice rose, Melissa. On the other hand, how about a beautiful swan? Or better yet, a fierce dragon for Brigid, to protect you from the evil world outside your doors. Oh! I could make us all little Napoleon hats. How about a bear? The Navajo believe the bear represents strength and power; it is considered one of the most important and sacred of animals. Did you know that some bears can hibernate up to seven months, while some don't hibernate at all?" While she spoke, Samantha acted out each offer—flapping her arms for the swan and growling for the bear.

Brigid grinned as Sam chattered on. She wondered how one person could have so much energy and know so much about so many things.

Sam continued her prattle, but Brigid was thinking about what she had said earlier. She was grateful that Sam wanted to protect her from the outside world, but she wondered if it was the other way around. *Does Sam feel safer in my company?* Brigid shook her head and decided it was another sign of the friendship that was blossoming between the two women.

Brigid treasured that closeness. They had spent a lot of time together, but Sam didn't tell her much about who she had left behind. Brigid didn't want to push her away with a lot of questions. Brigid learned more about her as she watched Sam interact with people in the store. She saw that Sam was a gentle, caring soul with an inner strength that impressed Brigid. She marveled at how far Sam had come from the woman walking the street reading a book in the rain, to this bright and happy woman.

Brigid recalled the day. She had been looking for Sam and found her in the children's section sitting in one of the armchairs with a small, brown-haired girl in her lap. The girl was four or five and was crying. Brigid listened to the conversation between the two.

"So, little princess, are you going to tell me, why the tears? Didn't you know that such pretty little girls should never need to cry?" Sam asked, as Brigid saw her smile at the child. Sam pulled a tissue out of her pocket and dried the little girl's tears.

"I got lost," the little girl said in a small voice. She looked up at Sam with pleading eyes. "I can't find my mommy."

"Well, that is serious. But it is something we can fix. I happen to be very good at saving princesses in trouble."

The girl looked up at Sam. "Can you help me?"

"Well, I will certainly try. Now the key to being lost is to stay where you are. That way when your mom comes to find you, you will be here, see?"

"I don't want to stay here all alone," she said with a quiver in her voice, tears rolling down her face.

"Well, that's a good thing," Sam said, drying the new tears with her fingers. "Because I was hoping I could stay while you wait, if that's okay?"

The girl nodded her head. "Yes, please," she said, settling closer into Sam's lap and chest.

Brigid watched the girl as she snuggled into Sam's lap. For a moment, she was envious of her, wishing she was the one. But then she felt guilty, as if she was betraying Tina.

"So, then the baby bear said, 'Someone's been eating my porridge and they ate it all up.' Now the bears were growing quite angry at the idea that someone had been in their house."

Brigid smiled and chuckled at the picture Sam and the child made. Sam looked up.

"Oh, Brigid, just the person we needed." she said with a big grin on her face and a quick tickle to the small girl on her lap. "It seems that my friend here has misplaced her mom. Could you help us find her?"

Sam turned to the little girl. "See, I told you if we stayed someone would find us, and they did."

Brigid leaned against the arm of the chair and looked down into Sam's eyes. A shiver traveled down Brigid's spine as Sam bared *her soul in that one look. Brigid glanced away, overpowered by the intensity of the moment.*

"Brigid? Are you okay?" Sam asked.

"Oh, yeah, sorry," Brigid said. "I was thinking how to handle the situation with your little princess here. Let's get her name and then I can make an announcement."

"Now that is why they pay you the big bucks, Brigid. You come up with the best ideas. I don't know why I didn't think of that." Sam turned to the little girl in her lap. "So, tell me, princess, what is your name?"

"My name is Annabelle Ballard."

"Well, Annabelle, let's see if we can find your mom." She stood up and put Annabelle on her shoulders. Annabelle giggled and held on as Sam walked to the front of the store.

Brigid shook her head of her memories. She could hardly believe the woman who sat so patiently then, was the ball of non-stop energy she saw now. She tried to pick up on what Sam was talking about. She hadn't missed much, but Brigid was soon lost as Sam jumped from topic to topic.

"Did you know that polar bears are the largest land predators? The biggest warm-blooded predator is the killer whale. And dragons...Chinese dragons are believed to be divine protectors and are the most vigilant. Hey, Melissa, how was your day so far?"

It was a second or two before Melissa answered. "Oh, pretty good. Rita and I had breakfast in the park in Greenport. The weather was great for it. That reminds me, though, I was wondering if you were busy on Saturday. I was hoping you could join us for a barbeque. My cousin Allison will be there. You met her the other day when she stopped in. I'm sure she would be happy to see you again."

"Melissa, are you trying to fix Sam up?" Brigid asked.

"Maybe, I don't know." Melissa shrugged. "Allison asked me to see if you could come, Samantha."

Brigid felt a pang of jealousy as she thought of Sam being with Allison.

"Gee, I don't know, Melissa," Sam said, the doubt and fear obvious in her eyes as she ran her hand through the hair on the back of her neck.

"Sam, I thought you wanted to come with me to my sister's this weekend," Brigid said before she knew what she was doing." "You know she is having a little family get-together for the kids sixth birthday. It won't be much...the kids, my mom, and David's family. You remember, right?"

"Oh, sure. I almost forgot. But are you sure?"

"Yes, I really mean it. I would love for you to come and meet everyone. Janet will probably take the kids down to the beach around noon, so, how about I pick you up at the motel around eleven?"

"Yeah, that would be great. I would love to meet them." Sam could barely contain her enthusiasm. Turning to Melissa she said, "Can I get a rain check on the barbeque?"

"Sure, Samantha. Maybe next weekend."

"Well, if I am going tomorrow, then I have to run some errands. I'll see you tomorrow, Brigid; eleven sharp, right?"

"Yeah." Brigid watched as Sam left the store. Once outside, Sam looked both ways, as if trying to decide where to go first. After a moment, she took off at a fast walk toward the motel.

Ellen Hoil

Chapter Seventeen

THE NEXT MORNING, BRIGID pulled up to Sam's room. Before she could turn off the engine, Sam was outside and ready to go. She was carrying a large, wrapped box, as well as a tall trash bag. Brigid got out of the car to help her.

"Hey, Sam. What is all this?"

"Well, I had to get the kids something. It's not polite to show up empty-handed."

"You didn't have to do that, Sam," Brigid said looking at the pile. "Uhm, we can try to fit the bag in the trunk with my stuff, but I think you're going to have to hold the box on your lap."

On their way to Janet's house, Brigid gave Sam the rundown of who would be there. Janet and David and the kids would, of course, but also Brigid's mother, and David's parents and sister. Brigid looked at Sam. She was listening to the music quietly playing on the radio, tapping her fingers on her knee along to the beat of the tune.

Sam placed her hand over Brigid's as it rested on the gearshift. Brigid tilted her head and was completely caught up in her eyes. Without thought, Brigid turned her hand over and entwined their fingers. She felt a tingle where they connected.

As she came to a stop in the driveway, Brigid closed her eyes and imagined running her fingers through Sam's fine hair. She knew it was something she would never—could never—bring herself to do without feeling a pain in her heart for Tina. She refused to allow herself to betray her memory like that. The sound of little fists tapping on her car window brought Brigid back to reality.

"Aunt Brigid, aren't you getting out?" Deidra yelled. "Mommy says we can't start without you. Hurry up!"

"Yeah, hurry up, Aunt Brigid!" Tyler tapped on the window again.

Brigid felt the loss when Sam pulled her hand away.

"I guess we'd better hurry up then." Sam said, and gave Brigid a large smile as she got out of the car and began collecting the packages.

As the women entered the backyard, Janet came to greet them.

"The kids said you had a guest." She held out her hand to Sam. "Hi, I'm Janet. Welcome to the party. I'm so glad Brigid brought you."

Janet looked at Sam from head to toe.

"Hi, Janet. I'm Samantha...Samantha Bailey," she said as she took Janet's hand. "It's a pleasure to meet you."

Brigid was stunned. It had taken her so long to even learn Sam's first name. Yet here she was sharing even more with Janet. Brigid looked on as the two interacted and was happy about the apparent new confidence Sam was finding. Janet was chattering on about the children, and Sam was paying rapt attention. Brigid's brows furrowed, as she stood behind Janet. She could see a glow in Sam's face and her blue eyes sparkle. From the warm and welcoming tone in Janet's voice she knew that she was trying to keep an open mind about Sam.

"Come over and sit with us at the picnic table." Janet said to Sam. "Mom is here along with Tracey, the rest should be here any minute though," As she sat down, Janet turned. "Come sit here next to me."

"Samantha, this is my mother, Katie Fitzpatrick, and David's sister, Tracey. This is my friend Samantha," Brigid said as she introduced everyone. After she sat, she leaned into the cooler next to the table and grabbed two bottles of beer. She looked at her friend, her eyebrow raised in silent question. Sam nodded and Brigid handed her the extra.

Brigid sat across from Sam and watched her closely. She wanted Sam to like her family and vice versa. As Brigid watched Sam and Tracey talk, she could see that Sam was as taken with Tracey as most people were. Tracey was an attractive woman. Brigid would concede that. Even Tina had not been blind to that fact. For some reason Brigid felt the same sense of jealousy. Confused, she looked into the open bottle. *I don't see why I should feel like this. Am I jealous? What do I have to feel jealous about? Sam and I aren't in a relationship. Not like Tina and I had.*

Brigid began to feel she was missing something. Some key piece of the puzzle that was linked to Sam. *Could it be that I have more feelings for Sam? Could this be more than a simple friendship? If it is, then what is it?*

Before she could come up with an answer, her attention was drawn back to the group as the conversations got livelier.

***

As the afternoon progressed, everyone relaxed, including Sam. She felt a sense of belonging for the first time in a long while. She reveled in it. While Sam and Janet chatted, Brigid's mother joined in.

"Tell me, Samantha, how did you meet our Brigid?" Katie asked.

"Oh, we sort of ran into each other outside the store one day. We had lunch together several times," Sam said, knowing that was a bit of a stretch on the truth.

"What do you do for a living?" Janet asked.

For an instant, Sam felt a fear creep in. She looked at Brigid and let Brigid's smile help relax her. She knew everything would be fine as long as her new friend was here with her.

"Well, right now I guess you could say I am between jobs. I'm an attorney, but I left my previous job and haven't begun looking for a new one yet," Sam said as she began to play with the bottle of beer picking at the label.

"She is helping me out at the store. She's a big help with the customers," Brigid said.

"How long have you been working at the store?" Tracey asked.

"Oh, only for a week or so. Before that I was just an avid reader." Sam smiled at Brigid. *I really want them to accept me. I need them to. Without them, how can I hope to gain what I want from Brigid?*

"So, you like to read. Well, you have that in common," Tracey said.

"Yeah, I could read all day given the chance." Sam nodded.

"Uhm, why did you leave your last job, Samantha?" Katie asked.

"I was unhappy with the work I was doing." Sam took a large gulp of her beer and began on the label again picking off large pieces of it now.

"Why?" Katie asked.

"I was a divorce attorney and the last case I worked on didn't end well, so I decided to quit." Sam's hands were clenched on the table. She could feel her anxiety begin to return.

"What happened?" Janet asked.

Sam took a deep breath and let it out slowly as she purposefully unclenched her hands and put them flat on the table. "Well, the mother I defended in a custody case was not someone I would want to have children, but my job forced me to overlook her unfitness and fight for her to have them, but they were all emotional basket cases." She looked down at the empty beer bottle and the pieces of label. She stared at them, but instead she thought back to the look on the children's faces the last time she saw them. "Can I have another bottle?"

Sam's fingers tapped on the tabletop. The motion got faster as she told more of the story. "The parents were so busy fighting over the kids that no one noticed how troubled they all were. You could tell they had been through hell. The oldest one was only ten and looked shell-shocked. I spent two days and nights working that case right before trial. When I realized she would win the case, I couldn't bear it. So, I quit. I handed my resignation to the managing partner. He agreed to buy me out. Then I left town"

When Sam finished her story, she looked down and noticed her nervous movement. She put her hands under the table. She looked up and saw an unknown expression in Janet's eyes. Sam could almost feel the heavy silence when she completed her tale.

"It's such a sad story," Katie said. "Those poor children."

"Do you ever plan on practicing again?" Tracey asked.

"I don't know. I haven't decided yet. It's one of the reasons I took off,"

"What do you mean 'took off?'" Janet asked, her voice holding a tone of suspicion to Sam's ears.

"Uhm, I left Illinois and came here." Sam frowned. "I took a road trip to try and quiet my mind. That didn't work out very well, though. But, being in town and working at the store have helped me feel more centered than I have in a while. It's given me a place to safely think things out." She smiled at Brigid. "I'm really grateful to Brigid for letting me hang out in the store to help now and then. It has saved me."

She hoped the truth she spoke was heard by Brigid. Without her Sam didn't know where she would be now. Certainly not sitting here. She longed for Brigid to know how much their friendship meant to her and how important it was. As far as Sam was concerned, it was a salvation. Though, as hard as she wished to express it, she felt paralyzed.

"I don't have any family anywhere, so leaving was easy." She said with little emotion in her voice.

"Oh, I'm so sorry to hear that," Katie said.

"It was a long time ago, and I think this is starting to feel like home. The town, the people, new friends." Sam looked around the table with her eyes coming to settle on Brigid's smile.

"Do you think you could settle here?" Tracey asked.

Sam continued to look at Brigid. "Well, I don't know. Whether I decide to settle down here or not depends on certain things."

"I'm sure we can find a good enough reason for you to stay." Brigid smiled.

"Then I guess I may be staying on."

"That would be wonderful."

Tyler and Deidra ran up to the table, breaking the spell that had formed between the two women. "Can we open our presents now?" they asked, jumping up and down.

"Not yet. We're still waiting for Grandma Susan and Grandpa Harry," Janet said.

The children switched their attention from their mother to Sam. She smiled.

"Did you bring us presents?" Tyler asked.

"Of course, I did. I wouldn't dream of coming to a party without gifts for the birthday boy and girl."

As Sam was speaking, the back gate opened, and an older couple came into the yard. As they came closer, a man Sam assumed was Janet's husband came out of the house carrying a plateful of uncooked hamburgers and hot dogs. He was as tall as the older man, but had the woman's looks.

"Grandma, Grandpa!" the kids yelled as they raced over to welcome them. The twins dragged the couple by their hands to the table.

"Look, Mom, they're here. Now can we open presents?" Deidra said.

"In a minute, honey. Let everyone get settled first." Janet admonished her with an indulgent smile.

Once everyone was around the table, Janet made the introductions. "Samantha, I would like you to meet my husband, David, his father, Harry, and David's mom, Susan."

"Hello, Samantha," Susan said.

With the introductions over. Drinks were filled and refilled. Everyone got comfortable around the table.

"Okay, now you can open the presents," Janet told the kids.

The children went at it full force. One present after another was opened, wrapping paper going every which way. When all the boxes were open, the kids took the time to see what booty they had received. They were ecstatic over Brigid's gifts, which went well with the Light Saber swords Tracey gave them. Apparently, this was a Star Wars birthday. There were Star War Lego sets, Tie-fighters and X-wing fighters, action figures, and other paraphernalia. Finally, the kids came to the big bag with the box inside that Sam had brought.

"Can we open it?" Tyler asked.

"Sure. Bring it here and let me help open it with you," Sam said with a big smile.

Tyler and Deidra dragged the bag over to Sam. Sam opened the bag and pulled out two large, wrapped boxes. She gave one to Tyler and one to Deidra. The two ripped off the paper and began yelling when they saw their Razor scooters.

"Yes!" Tyler yelled as he pumped his arm up and down.

"Oh, and there is one other gift. It was too big to fit in the car, so I got a tag for it at the store. You just have to go pick it up," Sam said to David with a smile. She handed the ticket to Janet. It was for a John Deere Farm Tractor Ride On.

"Oh, Samantha. This is too much. This must have cost you a fortune," Janet said.

"No, I wanted to, Janet. It was my pleasure. It's been a long time since I got to go to a toy store."

"I'm amazed," Janet said as she looked at the numerous gifts that Sam had brought "Though I don't know why you would go to so much trouble. It's enough that you wanted to come."

"And I have one more gift, but this is for the hostess." Sam reached for the box she had carried to the table and turned it over to Janet.

Janet unwrapped the box. The top of the box was embossed "Lenox."

"What have you done, Samantha?" Janet asked. She gasped when she opened the box and saw the small bud vase. A repeating leaf pattern climbed the sides of the vase and the top and bottom were gilded in gold, and small fleur-de-lis motif ran around the top. "Samantha, this is way over the top. I can't take this. It's more than I can accept."

Sam tilted her head. "Of course, you can. It's simply a little something I saw at the Outlet Center and thought you might like it. It is so beautiful. I thought you would love it."

"I do love it, and it is beautiful, but really it is too much," Janet said.

"Well, you have to take it, because it is bad luck to refuse a gift." Sam grinned.

"Okay, I'll keep it." Janet sighed. "But no more gifts. You have done too much between the kids and this."

"Okay, I promise. But you take all the fun out of it." Sam laughed.

The group spent the rest of the day visiting and watching the kids play with their toys. On several occasions Sam noticed Janet watching her. There was a look that Sam could only describe as puzzled on her face.

The twins became louder and louder as they ran around. As the noise progressed, so did Sam's speech pattern. She began to speak faster as the time passed, and her hands began to shake. Sam had no way to stop it. She only hoped no one noticed. *It's like I have no control over anything anymore.*

***

Toward the end of the day, Janet and Brigid found themselves separated from everyone else.

"I don't think I've seen anyone act the way she does. I find it curious," she said to Brigid. "Is Samantha the person you told me about that you met outside the store that day you found the package?"

"Yes, we've gotten to know each other since then. I'm glad we've become friends."

"How would you describe her overall personality?"

"Why do you want to know?" Brigid eyed her sister with a wary glance. "Seems a bit of an intrusive question."

"I'm just curious about the first person you've shown enough interest in to bring around here."

"Sam is gentle, caring, sweet, protective, and loyal. God, I sound like I'm describing a dog. But she is all that and much more. It's hard to describe, but for some reason, I feel safe around her. Now that I say it out loud, I haven't really felt that since Tina died. You just have to get to know her to get a true idea of who she is," Brigid said with a smile lighting up her face.

"What was she like when you first met her? I remember you saying you had a hard time getting her to talk to you."

"In the beginning she was very quiet. She spent most of her time walking around town and reading. She was shy and reserved. It took a lot of effort to get her to come into the store and talk to me. But now she's a great help. She talks to everyone and has made friends with Melissa and Stan, and some of the customers."

"She sounds like a remarkable person. I don't think I've seen you smile so much since Tina. Have you had any concerns about her? I mean, you've only known her a short time."

"You're starting to talk like you're my mother," Brigid said with a terse tone in her voice. "No, none. I mean, yeah, she was a little skittish at first, and she's been a little over enthusiastic at times, but I think everything is new to her.

"I don't know. Maybe it's just me being over-protective of my little sister." Janet put her arm around Brigid's shoulder. "Speaking of protective, what happened to the notes you were receiving?"

"Oh, I haven't received one in a while." Brigid frowned. "I hadn't thought about them since Sam started working at the store, she's kept me so busy. They stopped showing up...anyway, I haven't gotten another one, so I'm going to assume that whoever it was is done and has moved on."

"That is great news, sweetie. With any luck, whoever it was is gone for good. I really hope that's the case, for your sake, Brigid."

Brigid looked over and saw Sam chasing the kids around the yard. Brigid was happy that Sam got on well with them. The twins took an instant shine to her and they had played together most of the day. She watched as Sam appeared to suddenly withdraw into herself. She had walked to a quiet corner off by herself. It wasn't long before she recovered and became a central figure in the activities again.

"Well, Sam and I should be heading on home. I think your kids have worn her out enough for one day," Brigid said as she left the kitchen.

***

Sam was quiet for most of the car ride back to the motel. She looked out the passenger side window. *I think I did really well today. Everyone seemed to like me. I know I liked them. I did fine with the gifts I took. The children were great. I'm proud of myself for staying in control, especially that one time I was afraid I was losing it. I wish I could get into Brigid's thoughts...see what she's thinking right now. I mean, she did take me there. She wouldn't do that with just anyone. I guess there's only one way to find out. But, I'm sure she does.*

As they pulled into the parking lot of the motel, Sam turned to Brigid with a grin. She felt her own excitement like electricity that ran through her body.

Brigid got out of the car and went around to the passenger side, as Sam got out of the car and rested her arm on the open car door.

"I'm glad you went with me today. You made quite the impression on everyone, including me," Brigid said.

Brigid leaned closer to her and Sam felt like there was more Brigid wanted to say, but she didn't. Brigid took half a step back.

Sam looked into Brigid's eyes. *It feels right to be with her, to have her in my right now, here.* Before Sam realized she had moved closer,

Brigid leaned toward Samantha. Sam saw passion radiating from Brigid's eyes. She leaned in as well but slowly, so that Brigid had the chance to back out at the last moment. Not caring where they were, Sam kissed her. At first, the kiss was a gentle caress. But Sam put more pressure into the kiss. Sam's tongue begged entry, and Brigid gave it. Sam placed her arms around Brigid's waist and drew her closer. Sam moved her hand to the back of Brigid's neck, drawing Brigid deeper into the kiss. Both women moaned under the enveloping bliss.

Without any warning, Brigid broke away, pushing Sam back. "I can't do this. I'm sorry, I just can't. Tina..."

With that, Sam knew Brigid's heart would never belong to her. There would never be enough space for Sam to take Tina's place. Sam recognized there was nothing she could do to win Brigid's heart away from her past. With all the control and calm she could muster, as her own heart broke, Sam tried to console her.

"It's okay, Brigid, I understand. I've overstepped and I'm sorry. It won't happen again." Her heart was breaking, but she refused to let it show. "Let's put it down as a mistake and leave it at that."

"I'm sorry, Sam." Brigid lips trembled. "I never meant to hurt you by letting you think there could be more than our friendship. Being friends is all I'm capable of. I wish it could be more, but I don't know how it can. I can barely think right now."

"No, that's all right. It was my mistake." Sam let out a deep sigh. Trying hard to make Brigid think she was calm. "I guess I read more into it than there was. I hope we can still be friends?"

Sam could hear the desperate tone in her own question but was unable to keep it out. She shifted from foot to foot, hoping against hope not to hear the words she knew were coming, the words any potential lover didn't want to hear.

"Of course, we can." A weak smile crossed Brigid's lips. "I hope we can always be friends."

Sam felt her heart torn out. She knew she needed more than that and would never be able to achieve it. "Well then, I'll see you around," she said with a calmness she didn't feel.

"Sure, I'll see you at the store."

Sam unlocked the door to her room and turned back to Brigid, holding onto the door like it was a lifeline. "Yeah, I'll see you around." She closed the door, leaving Brigid alone in the parking lot.

***

That night the stranger stood outside Brigid's house looking up at the window to her bedroom. The light was on, despite the lateness of the hour. The stranger felt no need to hide in the woods anymore but stood in the shadows of the yard. The vigil would be kept, as it had been for what felt like forever. With no fear of being found, for now. The stranger knew it. The tenuous bond had to be kept. It was what the stranger would hold onto. Without it, all things known would be lost, set adrift with no anchor. She needed Brigid to act as the North Star for guidance and protection.

Finally, the light in the room went out. But the stranger remained until the coming of the dawn, when the light of day made it too dangerous to stay.

Chapter Eighteen

ALTHOUGH BRIGID WASN'T SCHEDULED to work, she went in anyway. She called Melissa and told her she could come in later. She needed something that would help her deal with her conflicting feelings and work helped her sort things out. She also wanted to be at the store for Sam. Brigid knew she hadn't been fair to her.

But Sam wasn't waiting for her. A feeling of dread set in. Her breathing increased and her heart felt heavy. She worried that what happened between them would keep Sam away. Tears began to fall from her eyes unnoticed. Brigid's stomach fluttered as she thought back to the kiss. *No kiss has felt like that, not since Tina. Who am I kidding, that was better than anything Tina and I shared.*

As Brigid opened the door to the store, she noticed the small piece of paper taped to the door. She looked all around the area as her heart rate sped up again but saw no one else. Brigid had grown accustomed to not seeing the notes anymore. Being alone made Brigid nervous as she reached for the paper as it flapped in the morning breeze.

> *Curse thee, Life, I will live with thee no more!*
> *Thou hast mocked me, starved me, beat my body sore!*
> *And all for a pledge that was not pledged by me,*
> *I have kissed thy crust and eaten sparingly*
> *That I might eat again, and met thy sneers*
> *With deprecations, and thy blows with tears,--*
> *Aye, from thy glutted lash, glad, crawled away,*
> *As if spent passion were a holiday!*
> *And now I go—Nor threat, nor easy vow*
> *Of tardy kindness can avail thee now*
> *With me, whence fear and faith alike are flown;*
> *Lonely I came, and I depart alone,*
> *And know not where nor unto whom I go;*
> *But that thou canst not follow me I know.*

This time Brigid recognized the writer—Edna St. Vincent Millay—but she couldn't remember the poem's title. Something in the back of her mind needled at her as she tried to remember the title of the poem.

"I'll look for it once I get settled." Brigid put the note in her pocket and instead let her mind drift to thoughts of Sam. "Geez, what am I going to do about her? I hope I didn't mess it all up yesterday." Her heart felt broken at the idea.

Brigid thought again of the note. The words of the poem were so angry and held such a sense of finality to them. Something about the idea of Sam and the note made her grow even more concerned about the situation.

Brigid tried to work on the idea while she moved over to the teapot and began the process of putting on the kettle for her morning tea. Her frustration got the better of her and she threw the pot in the sink. *I feel so helpless. If there was only something I could do. Anything. I should at least do something.*

"This has gone too damn far. This person who knows me well. But I can't even reach out in some sign of empathy." She took a calming breath and picked up the kettle again. "I know this person, I'm sure of it."

Brigid began to worry as the clock inched forward, ticking the minutes away, with still no sign of Sam, or clue about where she could be. She didn't think about the note, she was so focused on Sam. *Sam said she would be here, though she never said when. I just assumed it would be the same as always that she would be here waiting for me.*

Brigid still couldn't believe what happened the day before. She and Sam kissed. *I haven't kissed a woman like that since Tina. I hope I haven't ruined everything by pushing her away. Why did I act like that? Why did I then push her away? I wanted to kiss her. I wanted it as much as anything.*

Brigid spent the morning unpacking boxes of new books and putting them away and helping the few customers that came and went. It was busy work and she was able to think, and wonder, and worry. At one point, she reached into her pocket for a pen and touched the note. Her worry about Sam had pushed concerns about it and its author to the back of her mind. Now it became paramount. It was as if all the pieces all of a sudden fell into place. *Maybe if I knew more about the poem, I might be able to make sense of some of this. Sam, the letters and even maybe my own feelings.* Some feeling deep down in her soul told her it was important.

Brigid went to the literature section and picked up an anthology of Millay's works. She ran her finger down the index column at the back until she found the opening line. When she turned to the correct page and saw the title of the poem was *Suicide,* she felt more distressed. The bell over the door rang and Brigid jumped. She hoped it was Sam so they could talk about the note. She knew Sam would calm her nerves and help her sort through things. Instead of Sam, however, she saw her sister.

***

Janet met Brigid by the counter and immediately saw the worried look on her face and Brigid biting her lower lip.

"Brigid, what is it? Are you okay? And don't say 'nothing'. Is it about Samantha?"

"I don't know, Janet. I just don't know what to do," Brigid's voice rose in pitch as she held the crinkled note in her hand.

"Okay, calm down and tell me what happened." Janet put a hand on her sister's arm. "Together, we can try and work whatever it is out."

"I came to work this morning and found one of those notes again. I hadn't really thought about them for a while since I haven't gotten one in so long...at least not since Sam started opening the store with me and walking me out at night. Here, you read it." Brigid handed the crushed note to Janet. "Between this and Sam not coming in this morning, I'm worried. Something isn't right."

Janet read the note. "Brigid, this is serious. Where is Sam?"

"I told you, she wasn't here this morning when I opened up. I thought she would show up, but she hasn't. I think she's still upset about last night."

"Did something happen after you left my place? I thought things had gone well yesterday. Why would Samantha be upset?"

"It's my fault. When we went back to the motel, she kissed me,"

"She kissed you? And did you kiss her back?"

"Yes, no, I don't know. I stopped her once I realized what I was doing. It wasn't something I'd planned."

"Did you enjoy it?" Janet asked, her attention turning to Brigid for a moment.

"It was amazing. I think that's what scared me so much. I didn't know what to do. I was kissing her and then I thought of Tina. I was overwhelmed, confused, and even ashamed. We were kissing and I felt

83

like I was betraying Tina. So, I pulled back...Now, I think I was wrong. Maybe I should have let it happen. As much as I hate to face it, Tina is gone. I need to accept that fact."

"What did you say to her? How did she react?" Janet asked.

"I told her that it couldn't be that way between us. But that I hoped we could remain friends. She agreed to forget it. When we said goodbye, she said she would be here. I assumed she was okay. Perhaps I was wrong."

"Don't worry, Brigid, you'll get a chance to apologize. Maybe you'll see her later, or tomorrow." Janet muttered under her breath, "This is not good".

"What?" Brigid asked.

"Brigid, do you think it's possible Samantha took it a bit harder than you imagine. What room is she staying in at the motel?"

"Eleven. Why? Are you going over there?"

"Yeah. Since you're stuck here, I think I'll go check on her. Make sure everything's okay."

Janet appeared unconcerned, but Brigid could tell by the slight tightness in her small smile that there was something Janet was keeping from her. Especially since she appeared to not want to take Brigid with her.

"I'll go with you. If any fences need mending, I want to be there to do it."

"I think you should stay here. Why leave the store. I'll give you a call when I talk to her."

Brigid gave her sister a determined look.

"Fine. Years of working as a nurse in the ER has taught me to read people enough to know there is no way to stop you."

"Let me have two minutes to lock up. I'll call Melissa from the car."

Chapter Nineteen

THE TWO PULLED UP to Sam's room at the motel. The room was dark, and the curtains were drawn. Brigid knocked on the door several times but got no answer.

"Maybe she's sleeping, or in the shower. Sam, it's Brigid. Can I talk to you?" she called. "Sam, it's important. Please come to the door."

"Could she have left, or checked out?" Janet asked

"I don't think so. I'm pretty sure that's her car," Brigid said, pointing to an expensive sports car.

Janet peeked through the small opening between the drawn curtains. "I think I see some movement. I'm going to ask the manager if we can get in there. You stay here in case she shows up or answers the door."

"If she's in there, why isn't she answering the door? Maybe she's too mad to talk to me, but Sam would have the courtesy to come to the door." Brigid pounded on the door again.

Janet shook her head as she walked away. *I should've told her what I thought was going on with Samantha last night. Now I can only hope to talk to Samantha first.* Janet jogged across the parking lot to the motel office. The manager sat behind the counter, feet propped on his desk, watching a soap opera on the television.

"Excuse me, can you help me?" Janet asked.

"What can I do for you, miss?" the man asked as he stood up and came around the counter.

"I'm looking for the manager, or someone who can help me get into one of your rooms."

"Well, I'm the manager. What room do you need to get into and why?" His brow furrowing.

"A friend of mine is in room eleven and she isn't answering the door. I think she may be sick. I'm a nurse and I want to make sure she's okay."

"How do I know that you really are her friend and not some stranger trying to get access to one of my guests?" He looked Janet over.

"Your guest in room eleven is Samantha Bailey...blonde, blue eyes, about five ten, or five eleven, usually has a book in her hands."

"Yeah, that's her, but that still doesn't get you in the room. I don't just let people into guests' rooms. If she wanted you in there she would let you in."

"Look, sir, I know this is unusual, but I really believe my friend may be in trouble. She wasn't feeling well yesterday, and now she isn't coming to the door. I want to check on her. You can stay and watch if you're that worried about letting me in."

"Let me get the key and we can go take a look," he said after a moment. He reached under the counter and pulled out a giant set of keys.

As they walked across the parking lot, Janet saw Brigid still banging on the door, calling out for Samantha. When Brigid got no answer at the door Janet saw her try to peek through the curtains.

"Brigid, I've got the manager. He's going to let us in." Janet said as they walked up.

The man went to the door and looked for the right key.

"I can't thank you enough for this, sir," Brigid said, the anxiety in her voice evident.

"Dennis, Dennis Fowler," the man said, still looking for the key. He picked one and looked at it. Janet couldn't imagine how he could keep them straight enough to know the right one. But when he put it in the lock and turned it the door opened.

Brigid started inside but Janet held her back by the arm. "Wait."

"Wait? Wait for what? Sam could be in there sick or hurt. Why wait?"

"No, Brigid, really, please. Wait out here for a minute while I go check on her. If she is sick, she probably doesn't want you to see her, and if she's hurt, I need someone out here to call for help. Okay? I'm sure she's fine, but I want to look first, okay?"

"All right, but only for a minute." Brigid crossed her arms over her chest, her hands tucked in tight.

Janet recognized the stance. Brigid used it to calm herself down ever since she was a child. "Okay." Janet squeezed Brigid's shoulder before she sighed and approached the door. Her palms grew sweaty, she felt more nervous than she should be. Janet was afraid of what she would find. *If I am right, please, God, give Brigid and Samantha the strength to handle this together.*

Janet stepped into the dark room. The television had been overturned, the bedding was all over the room, and the mattress was laying half off the frame and on the floor. In contrast to the chaos, books were piled neatly in the corners and along the walls. However, what was quick to catch Janet's attention, were the photographs taped to the wall over the bed. Pictures of Brigid—all of them.

"Well, that answers one mystery." Janet didn't take the time to examine them since her only concern at this point was Samantha.

Janet tried to turn the light on using the switch by the door, but nothing happened. She couldn't open the curtains because of the mattress and books. Using only the light from the door, Janet searched the shadows. She heard a keening noise, like that of an injured animal, on the other side of the bed. Samantha was curled up on the floor, her hands covering her ears, and crying.

Not a good sign. "Samantha," Janet said in a hushed voice as she walked around the bed. "Samantha. Samantha, it's Janet, Samantha."

Samantha did not respond as Janet bent down and laid a gentle hand on Samantha's back. She moved her hand in gentle circles, like she did with the twins after a nightmare. Samantha didn't shy away, but still keened and continued to cover her ears so tight the back of her hands were white.

"Samantha, do you want to tell me what happened?"

Samantha stopped and looked up at Janet, her eyes filled with tears. "Can you make the TV shut off? I've tried everything but the sound won't turn off. Can you make it stop, please?"

Janet's fears were realized. Samantha was in a delusional state. Janet knelt next to her in the quiet room. "Sure, honey, we can make it stop." *This is worse than I thought.* "Is the TV or someone else talking to you, Samantha?" *Please say no, Samantha, please.*

"No. Just make it stop. I want to go to sleep. It's been so long, but I can't with all the noise. I tried, Janet, honest I tried."

"Samantha, do you remember the last time you slept?" Janet asked after a quick sigh of relief that Samantha didn't think the TV was talking to her.

"The day before yesterday, or maybe before that, I can't think, everything is so fast in my mind."

"Okay, honey, we're going to help you get some sleep, but you have to come with me, sweetie. We have to go outside. If we go outside I can help you. I can take you somewhere where we can make the noise stop. I promise."

Samantha jumped up against the wall, knocking over several piles of books. "No, I won't go. I don't want to leave here, everything I need is here," Samantha said, raising her voice and pointing to her books. "Make the noise stop and everything will be fine. I swear, I won't do it again." She pointed to the wall over the bed before putting her hands back over her ears.

"Samantha, I can't do that here. We need to go somewhere else," Janet said as she stood up and tried to approach her.

Samantha pinned herself against the wall, pulling a small pocketknife off the nightstand. "I told you, Janet, I don't need to go. Just fix the fucking TV!" she screamed. "Please."

***

Brigid waited outside with Mr. Fowler. *What could possibly be going on in there?* She paced back and forth in front of the door.

What does Janet think she is going to find in there that Sam wouldn't want me to see? If Sam is sick, I would think she would want my help. Brigid wrought her hands trying to remain calm. Brigid couldn't see anything going on in the room. She tried to look without getting too close. *I have to let Janet handle this. I trust her. Sam will be fine, I'm sure of it.*

Brigid stepped away with a deep sigh, frustrated. She continued pacing before leaning against the minivan, wrapping her arms against herself. *After last night, I wouldn't blame her if she didn't want to see me again. Could she be mad at me? I don't think so. I hope not. She seemed so okay when I left. I know it was the coward's way out, but I had to leave. I was so confused.*

Brigid glanced at Mr. Fowler, who watched in silence, running his hand though his sparse hair. She began playing with the rear-view mirror, flipping it back and forth.

I wasn't strong enough to stay. I hadn't been kissed like that since Tina died. It was amazing. Too amazing. It scared me. I felt at home in Sam's arms, and when we kissed, my soul felt at peace and safer than I've ever felt.

I was so overwhelmed. I was shocked that I felt that deeply for someone again. I did the only thing I knew how to do. I tried to ignore it and pretend it never happened. But it did happen, and now Sam is in there. Is she angry, hurt, or sick because I walked away? I wouldn't blame her, but I only want to tell her how she made me feel for the first time in a long time. I felt something other than the loneliness and emptiness I've lived with for so long. I felt love.

Brigid pushed off the car and walked back toward the room. *Did I say 'love?' I can't love her. I've only known her a few weeks. How could I possibly even think I love her? I haven't felt this way about anyone for so long. She makes me feel the way Tina did, and last night it felt like more.* Brigid stopped her short trek. *Oh, my God, what am I going to do?*

The longer Brigid waited, the more worried she was about Sam and about her own confusing feelings. She knew that what seemed like hours was only a few minutes. When she heard Sam scream, she rushed into the room. Sam was pressed up against the wall. She looked like a frightened child.

"Sam, you're okay. We came to see if you're okay," Brigid said, as she started to step closer. "What's the matter, Sam? What's going on? Are you all right? Please, answer me, you're starting to scare me."

Janet grabbed Brigid by the shoulder. "Brigid, wait. Samantha isn't well. Why don't we step outside and we'll get Samantha some help?"

"Why?" Brigid looked back at Sam. There was a wildness in Sam's eyes Brigid didn't recognize. Brigid realized that Sam barely recognized them. She also saw the knife in Sam's hand.

"Janet? Sam? What's going on?" She asked as she looked between one and the other. She was shocked at what she was seeing. How did Sam become this stranger? Gone was the strong, confident person she was yesterday, replaced with this frightened, wild being. "Someone tell me what's happening here," she said, her voice an octave higher than normal.

"Let's step outside, sweetie, and I'll explain everything. We'll give Samantha a chance to calm down." Janet took Brigid by the arm and led her outside. Brigid looked over her shoulder as they left.

***

Once Janet and Brigid left, Sam threw the knife away as if it burned her. Sam shook her head and covered her ears as the noise made it hard for her to think. She looked up and around the room. She took in the bed, the books, the TV, and finally the knife laying on the floor where she threw it. Her brows furrowed deep, and she felt her jaw clench. *What the hell just happened?*

Ellen Hoil

Chapter Twenty

BRIGID WATCHED AS JANET made a call on her cell phone. *What is going on here? What could possibly be wrong with Sam? She looked crazed. Is she on drugs or alcohol?*

"I called an ambulance," Janet said as she slid her phone back in a pocket. "Samantha needs medical attention. I convinced them we didn't need police help since I'm an ER nurse."

"Why would we need police? What is wrong with her, Janet?" Brigid's hands trembled and her eyes grew teary. "She barely recognized us."

"She did, Brigid. She knew you were there...you have to believe that. If anything, believe that."

"Don't tell me bullshit, Janet. She looks like a scared animal, for God sake. Is it drugs or alcohol?"

"No, it's not that, Brigid. I'm sorry but we have to wait to find out what's truly happening to her."

Brigid wasn't happy with the answer but gave in to her sister's professional demeanor. She knew Janet was taking this very seriously, which only made Brigid worry more.

When the ambulance arrived, Janet spoke to the two attendants. "I think I can coax her out, but I would advise you guys to be ready. If I can't, we can call for backup then."

Brigid realized, if they couldn't get Sam out of the room calmly, there was a chance she would be treated as a criminal and dragged out. She didn't know if she could bear to watch that. She ran past everyone into the motel room. Just inside the door, she stopped and looked for Sam.

Sam was curled up against the wall, her head in her hands. Brigid stood in front of her.

"Sam, it's me. I want you to come outside with me."

Sam looked up at her with bloodshot eyes. "Go away, Brigid, you can't do anything here now. It's too late. The damage is done. Can't you see that? Can't you see what I've become?" She laid her face in her hands again, but not before Brigid saw the tears streaming down her cheeks.

Brigid kneeled and placed a comforting hand on Sam's head. "I can't, Sam. You mean too much to me. We can work through this together, whatever it is. Please, Sam, for me, walk outside with me." Brigid held out hand.

"Can I deny her this one last thing? After today I will never see her again, I'm sure of it," Sam said as though Brigid wasn't there. Sam looked up at Brigid. "She is as beautiful as ever. I will always remember the way she looked, the way she felt in my arms, how sweet her lips tasted."

"Sam, why do you think we'll never see each other again? I'll always be here for you, I promise."

Sam stood up, using the wall to support herself. Her gaze never meeting Brigid's eyes.

Brigid held her hand out again to her. "Come on, Sam, it'll be okay. You'll see."

Sam took her hand and let Brigid lead her from the room into the parking lot. Brigid felt Sam hesitate as they stepped into the sunshine. The ambulance was parked directly in front. Brigid looked up at her and watched as fear once again washed over Sam's face. She squeezed her hand,

"It's okay, Sam. They have to do it this way. You'll be fine," she said in a soft voice, almost a whisper.

Sam looked down and their eyes met. Brigid gave her a small smile to try and offer some comfort. After a moment, Sam stood up straight and squared her shoulders. "I'm ready."

Together they walked toward the ambulance. Brigid saw Janet's jaw drop open and then close again and raised an eyebrow as she walked over to meet them.

"Samantha, do you think you can stay calm for a while?" Janet asked in a gentle tone.

"I think so." Sam said. Her voice quiet and trembling.

One of the attendants pushed the gurney toward Sam. She looked at it and then at Janet. "Can you stay with me?" Sam asked Brigid as she lay down on the gurney.

Brigid sensed Sam's fear growing and took her hand. As she began to walk alongside the moving stretcher, she saw Janet shaking her head.

"It's going to be okay, Sam," she said with as reassuring a smile as she could muster. "Janet is going to ride with you. Right, Janet?"

"Right."

"And I'll be right behind you in the car. I promise." Brigid gave Sam's hand one final squeeze before she let go. She watched as the men loaded Sam into the ambulance. Janet climbed in and took a seat next to her. Brigid could see her talking to Sam when the doors closed behind them. The last thing she saw was Sam looking at her.

Brigid stood in the parking lot and watched the ambulance drive off. The white van with its flashing lights, shrunk in the distance. Her vigil was broken by the sound of Mr. Fowler clearing his throat.

"I'm sorry about your friend, miss, but what am I supposed to do about the room? It's paid for till the end of the month, but there is a lot to clean up in there."

"Don't worry, Mr. Fowler, I'll take care of cleaning up the room. Just give me a day. My name is Brigid Fitzpatrick. Here's my card" She stared down the road as she reached in her purse and took out one of her business cards.

After a moment Brigid returned to the room. She looked at the destruction, amazed that Sam had so much self-hate and turmoil in her. As she turned to leave, the wall behind the bed caught her attention. She walked closer to get a better look. The pictures were of her. Some had been taken in front of the bookstore. More shots were taken through the windows at her house. There were some of her in the backyard playing with Artemis and on the beach with Janet and the kids. Brigid felt weak in the knees. Brigid was confused. *When were these taken? I've never seen Sam with a camera. How did she do this?*

Brigid grabbed the nightstand for support. It wasn't just the harmless notes, it was everything. Brigid caught the glimmer of the sun as it reflected off the knife left behind. *Would she have hurt me? Could it have gone that far?*

Ellen Hoil

Chapter Twenty-one

BRIGID DROVE TO THE hospital on automatic pilot. *How is it possible that Sam is the stalker I've been so afraid of? How could I not have noticed anything? There must have been signs. How could I have been so stupid? Falling for all the lies she told me, only so she could get close to me.* She slammed her hand on the steering wheel and grimaced at the sting it caused.

But the lies seemed so real, so sincere. How could you do this to us, Sam? When I looked into your eyes or felt your touch, it didn't feel fake or false, it felt honest. More honest than anything I've felt in such a long time. Can I stand to be with you now? How can I not? She appeared so lost and afraid. At the hotel she looked more scared and in pain than anything else. I'm so fucking confused.

When Brigid arrived at the hospital's emergency room, she asked for Sam at the front desk, only to be told that she would have to wait. She wasn't family, so Brigid knew she couldn't force her way in to see Sam. In a way, Brigid was a bit relieved. *Somehow, I know seeing Sam right now would only make me mad again. Why did she do it? I don't understand. Why? What did she want from me?*

Brigid spent the next two hours thinking about Sam. To clear her mind and let her anger dissipate, she walked around the first floor of the hospital simply following the lines on the floor. *I wonder how she's doing now? How are they treating her? I hope she's not all alone in some cold, impersonal room. Maybe Janet is keeping her company? Why do I care so much what they are doing to her? I don't know why I'm even here. After everything she has put me through the last few weeks, I am the last person who should be here.*

But no matter her rationalization for leaving, Brigid stayed. Walking around, she passed through the ER a few times. When she did, she asked if there was any word yet. After a while, the walking wasn't doing anything to relieve her and she took a seat in the ER waiting room.

Brigid jumped up when she saw Janet come through the ER doors. She had a serious, professional expression on her face. Janet motioned for Brigid to sit back down as she sat next to her. Brigid wrung her hands as she waited for Janet to say something. After a moment of nothing, Brigid couldn't stand the silence anymore.

"What's going on, Janet? Can I see her? I need to talk to her. I want to know why...you know what she did, you saw that room too."

Janet looked up at her sister. "No, you can't see her right now, Brigid. I'm sorry. The only reason they let me in with her was because she asked for me and I work here. Right now, another nurse is with her. I'll go back when we're done. Don't worry, someone is with her."

"She didn't ask for me? Janet, what's wrong with her? She was acting so bizarre. It scared me to see her like that. And then there were all the pictures. What was she doing following me like that? I thought she was my friend. What kind of friend would do that? For that matter, what kind of person would do that?"

Janet looked away for a moment before again looking up at Brigid. "I'm sorry, honey, but I can't tell you that."

"You don't know what is wrong with her? Janet, you must have some idea. Please tell me."

"Please sit down, sweetie." Brigid sank into her. "I can't tell you, Brigid, I'm not allowed to. The only one who can do that is Samantha herself. I'm sorry."

"Why, Janet, why would she do it?"

Janet looked Brigid in the eye and took hold of her hands. "I wish I could tell you that, Brigid. I really do. I will tell you that if it was me, I'd wait to talk to her before I made any judgments."

Brigid pulled away. "I don't understand. Can someone let me know what to do? Because a large part of me wants to go in there screaming at her, telling her I'm going to the police." She took a deep breath. "But another part of me wants to understand why she did it and beg her for a reasonable explanation that will make this all better. But right now, I think the loud part is too strong to be reasonable. Right now, I don't know if I can forgive her for what she has put me through. I don't think I'm capable of deciding what to do."

The two women sat in silence. Minutes passed by. "Is she going to be okay? I mean, it's nothing life threatening or anything, right?" Brigid finally asked, as she looked at the wall in front of her instead of at Janet. Her voice was low and soft. Afraid of the answers.

"No, she'll be fine. She may have to stay in the hospital for a little while, depending on what the specialist says, but I am positive she can beat this. I have faith that Samantha is made of stronger stuff than you or I could imagine."

Brigid looked in Janet's eyes and saw the belief she had in her statement. "I wish you could give me the answers I need to come to some kind of terms with this. Even if only a small part of it."

Janet remained quiet. She took Brigid's hand and gave it a squeeze. "I wish I could, too," she whispered.

"I don't know what to do, Janet. I'm confused and hurt right now." Her voice rose with each sentence. "I feel betrayed. She was my friend. Was her friendship a lie? She knew I was scared of the pictures. Why didn't she say anything? Was everything we shared a lie? Tell me what I should believe."

"I can't, Brigid. The only one who can explain is Samantha herself. They are answers you will have to wait for. I'm sorry. I know I keep saying it, but I truly do wish I could help you."

"You're my sister, Brigid, my flesh and blood. I care deeply for you, you know that. But it isn't up to me to tell you. Samantha will have to when she is able. Why don't you go home? Have some rest. You've been here all day and I know you're physically and emotionally drained. Take the van and go home. I'll be awhile. I can get a ride home."

"Are you sure I can't see her?"

"Yes, I'm sure. She is going to be a while longer, and even then I can't promise that she will be able to see you today."

"But she will see me when she can, right?"

"I don't know, Brigid. I pray that she does."

"I guess I'll go home then. I could use a good night's sleep. Maybe tomorrow this will all begin to make sense to me, and I can decide what to do." Brigid stood up to leave. "If you see her, can you tell her that I lo...that I hope she feels better."

Ellen Hoil

Chapter Twenty-two

STILL IN HER STREET clothes, Sam laid on the bed in the ER. When she first came, a woman she hoped was a doctor gave her a shot of what she was told was Haldol. Sam didn't care what it was, it made the noises and voices go away. Whether they would come back she didn't know. The thought scared her. She was worn out, whether from the drug or maintaining a hold on herself she wasn't sure

Sam was exhausted. She had been restrained on the bed since she came in and taken off the ambulance gurney. Janet stayed with her, either holding her hand, or just being nearby. When Janet stepped out of the room a nurse had come in to take her place sitting in the chair by the wall. Being constantly watched, even by someone she trusted, was starting to make her feelings of suspicion rise again. Even though the restraints were lined with a soft material they were still uncomfortable. The restraints were connected to the metal rails of the bed and they were having an effect on her mood.

Sam had spent a lot of energy and felt defeated. Being restrained for so long wore on her already frazzled thoughts. The frustration grew as she tried to squeeze her hands free. She thrashed about trying to get the shackles off. But it did nothing but make one of the nurses come to check that the ties were still secure.

Sam wanted nothing more than to go home and sleep. If she slept, she wouldn't have to think about Brigid.

"How can I ever explain what I did to her? By now she knows what I did. I know I'll never see her again." She let out a deep sigh. "It would have been nice to at least get the chance to say goodbye. Nothing I say can make up for all the stress I've put Brigid through."

Sam forgot she was not alone and was startled when Janet spoke from her spot across the room.

"I can only imagine how it feels right now, Samantha." Janet walked over the side of the bed and laid her hand on top of Samantha's and gave it a gentle squeeze. "You have to realize, though, that while you may think what you did was scary and unforgivable, it wasn't. Once

Brigid realizes what happened, she'll come to understand you meant no harm. Nothing you did was that bad that it can't be fixed." Janet gave her hand one more squeeze and let go.

Sam was so deep in thought she didn't notice the doctor enter the room holding her chart until Janet stepped away.

"Hello, Miss Bailey. How are you feeling now that you've had some time?" He didn't look up from the notes on the chart. "My name is Dr. Johnson. The ER doctor who saw you first has asked me to talk to you. We need to assess your current state. I see that, aside from being agitated when you came in, you were also hearing voices, and you pulled a knife during an altercation. Is that correct?"

"I already explained this."

"I understand, but I just need to hear it from you directly."

Sam noticed he didn't make eye contact with her. It was making her angry and frustrated all over once more. "It wasn't a real knife, only a small pen knife." she said in a terse tone. "And I didn't 'pull it' on anyone. I happened to have it in my hand, and the 'altercation' wasn't much either." She hoped that playing the whole thing down would help her get her out of there. *I'm fine now, why can't they see that, instead of wasting everyone's time.*

Dr. Johnson looked at her and Samantha could tell he didn't believe her. "Nurse Shelly said you picked up the knife during her attempt to talk to you. She also said you wrote a disturbing note this morning."

"It wasn't a 'disturbing note.' It was a bit of poetry I copied from a book. That's all it was." Sam hoped she could talk her way home. The doctor seemed to be making a lot more out of it than there was.

"And what about the voices?" Dr. Johnson asked with a raised eyebrow, looking directly at Sam. The skepticism on his face told Sam he was going to be difficult.

Why doesn't he just believe me? "They weren't voices. I think it was a TV or radio, maybe from one of the rooms next door." Sam looked the doctor directly in the eyes, defying him to question her explanation.

Dr. Johnson gave a vague nod. "Right. When you came in you were agitated. Can you tell me what that was about?" He scribbled notes on the chart.

"It was nothing. I had a disagreement with a friend of mine, and I hadn't had any sleep. I got a little upset. Nothing more." Each question made Sam more aggravated. "Look, I don't know what you want from me. Why can't I simply go home? I only need to get some sleep. That's all I need. Get some sleep and maybe talk to my friend and I'll be fine."

But Brigid won't talk. Not after what I did today. Not after everything I've done.

"From what Nurse Shelley said, you got a little more than upset in your motel room," Dr. Johnson said, shattering Sam's self-diagnosis.

"Look, if it is a matter of paying the damages, I am sure I can work out something with the manager. I was angry. I threw a few things. Nothing serious happened. I can fix it. I'm sure I can fix it. Nothing happened that can't be fixed."

Sam didn't need any complications, but the doctor was pushing her buttons. She decided to take a break from his inquisition and turned away and faced the wall to her right, trying to get lost in the pattern of the tiles. She sniffled and tears escaped from her eyes. *Except for Brigid. I can never fix that. I just wish...if I could only explain. If I could see her.* Sam let a deep sigh escape her. She knew it would never happen. She couldn't ask for forgiveness for the unforgivable pain she caused. She gave one more pull to the restraints, and realized, again, that she was trapped.

"Well, be that as it may, I would like to see you stay for a little while, so we find out what caused your agitated state and how you respond to the medication we will be giving you. We will put you on a prescription, but I want you to stay here so we can see any adverse reactions you may have to it."

"For how long?" Sam asked, dejected and exasperated at the thought of staying overnight.

"Two, maybe three, weeks, if you agree" he said matter-of-factly, never looking up from her chart.

Sam's mouth dropped open. "Two to three weeks?! No way! I have to get out of here. Now!" she yelled at him, pulling harder at the bands holding her to the bed.

"I'm sorry, Samantha, but that won't be happening, at least not tonight, or tomorrow. From what I understand, you are here alone. Because of that, I'm recommending that we keep you here for the full seventy-two hours we are allowed. During that time, I'm hoping we can help you get more stable. After that I would suggest you consider staying longer. It can only benefit you in the long run by giving our staff and yourself time to get you on the path to long-term treatment. Regardless, I would like you to stay until we can be sure you will be safe." Dr. Johnson looked up from the chart with a serious, but reassuring, look on his face, as if that would make the news easier to take.

"It won't happen again. I told you that." Sam attempted to sit up, but she was still held by the restraints around her wrists. She laid back, seething in anger. "Are these things really necessary?" She gave the restraints a jerk.

Dr. Johnson looked at her, his eyes softening for the first time since he came in. "Yes, I am afraid it is hospital procedure. It's for your own protection. Once we get you admitted into a room, we can take them off."

"Well, you can take them off now because I'm not staying."

"Miss Bailey, let me be honest with you about this." Dr. Johnson sat on the metal stool next to Sam's bed and looked directly into her eyes, his dark blue scrubs contrasted against the white lab coat he wore. "As I've told you, there really is no choice for you at this point. We can check you into the hospital tonight, without your permission. Based on the details of the incident this morning we have the right to admit you without your consent, because you are either a threat to yourself or to others. If we do that, you'll have to remain here for at most seventy-two hours, or less if we decide it's safe for you to leave. Once we get you started, I hope you will seriously consider staying longer by choice. It can only help you in the long-term. We really do want to help you, Samantha."

"I don't understand any of this. How can you keep me here against my will? It was simply a misunderstanding." Sam's voice mirrored her frustration. "Look, what if I do outpatient? I could come by and check in every day. You could do what you need and then I could go home. I promise to show up tomorrow."

"I'm sorry, Miss Bailey, but without anyone outside the hospital to take care of you, this is the only alternative we can offer at the moment. Do you have anyone you could stay with after you are discharged?"

"No, at least not anymore," she said in a whisper.

"There is no way around this then. We will be admitting you tonight. The choice of what happens then is entirely up to you."

Sam knew she wasn't really being given any choice at all. She didn't know what to think. Her mind felt fuzzy. Likely from the drugs they had given her. Sam knew she could fight it legally, but that would take time. *I could stay a few days, figure out what to do next.*

Sam studied the striped curtain hanging in front of her bed as she thought about her predicament. She turned back to the doctor and looked him over with a critical eye to gauge whether or not he would keep her there. What she found in his manner gave her little hope.

"So, if I admit myself after then, I can leave anytime I want?"

"Yes, any time after the first seventy-two hours."

"Okay, it looks like I have little choice. I'll take the lesser of two evils and leave when I'm ready to go." Sam sighed and turned her head away again.

"All right. I need you to sign these papers." Dr. Johnson placed a pen in her fingers and held the chart for her. "Sign on the bottom of the second page after you read it through."

"Just turn the damn thing and let me get this whole damn thing over with." After the doctor flipped up the top page, she signed without bothering to read it. *It's not like anyone will notice I'm gone or miss me. Not anymore, at least.* Sam felt the pen taken out of her hand as she stared up at the ceiling. She barely heard the doctor as he said someone would be in soon to take her upstairs to her room.

Ellen Hoil

Chapter Twenty-three

AFTER SEVERAL HOURS IN the emergency room, Sam was taken to her floor by an orderly. A nurse greeted them at the door. Sam felt overwhelmed and barely looked at her. Fear began to set in when she heard a second set of solid doors click and lock behind them as the orderly wheeled her bed past the doors. Here she was tied to a bed with no way of getting out. *What if they don't let me leave?* Her panic built the further into the ward they went. *This is the psych ward.* Samantha took a deep breath, hoping her fear didn't show. But the realization of where she was, and what she had agreed to, set in. *What the hell am I going to do? I've signed my life away.*

The orderly pushed her bed into one of the rooms down the long corridor. The walls were painted white at the bottom with the top half painted sky blue. From her position on the bed, Sam couldn't see much around her, but she heard voices down the hallway and in the rooms.

The room they took her into was completely tiled and reminded Sam of a gym locker room. She saw a set of open showers with a tile wall separating the stalls. There was nothing else in the room except a medical supply cabinet and hooks on the walls.

The nurse came around and untied Sam from the bed. "Hi, my name is Mrs. Fogarty."

Sam rubbed her wrists where the ties had been. "Thanks. I was beginning to feel like they would never come off."

The nurse was an older woman with salt and pepper hair. Sam guessed her to be around sixty. She had a friendly smile and warm eyes. Sam took a deep breath feeling a bit reassured.

"I know. It can be a bit much. Okay, dear, I need you to strip out of your clothes. We need to check you out and then you can take a nice shower," Mrs. Fogarty said.

"Check me out? You mean a physical? Isn't that what being downstairs was about?" Sam's brow furrowed in confusion. She didn't understand why she needed a physical in the shower room.

"We will take your vitals and weigh you when you're done with your shower. But before that, we have to do a body search. I'm sorry. I know it sounds like too much, especially after what you've been through, but it is procedure. We've had people try and sneak things onto the floor before."

"Is that really necessary? I promise I don't have anything on me. They took all my personal effects downstairs."

"I am sorry, sweetie, but it is required of all new patients here. I'll make this as fast and easy as I can for you. Please relax and cooperate, and it will be over before you know it," Mrs. Fogarty said. "Otherwise I'll have to ask for someone to come help us. I don't think either of us wants that to happen."

Sam realized the exam would happen, regardless of what she wanted, no matter how degrading. She stiffened in anticipation of what was to come next. Sam took off her clothes, carefully hanging each piece on the hooks on the wall. She realized the tiles were the same hue as the blue walls in the corridor and the ER. She wasn't sure why she noticed that, other than a way to not focus on what was going on. Sam jumped at the sound of a latex glove being snapped on. She turned in time to see Nurse Fogarty putting lubricant on her fingers.

"Okay, dear, let's get the worst of this over with, and then it will all be easy after that. Just relax and it will be over in a moment."

Sam tried to shut down as she felt the nurse's fingers begin their invasion. The nurse placed a comforting hand on Sam's back, rubbing it a bit. Sam tried to think of something calming and soothing. Trying to ignore the feel of latex against her back, she pictured Brigid laughing with a sparkle in her chocolate colored eyes and it helped her relax. Samantha was so lost in the sight of Brigid's face that she didn't notice the nurse was finished until she was standing in front of her with no gloves on.

"Now, I need you to open your mouth." Samantha did as she was told while the nurse looked in her mouth. "You go take your shower now. We have plenty of hot water, so try and relax. I'll have something for you to put on when you're done."

Sam looked at the shower and then back at Mrs. Fogarty, waiting for her to leave. When the nurse made no move to leave, Samantha arched an eyebrow.

"I'm sorry, honey, but I have to stay. You have to be supervised."

"Supervised? Why? Do you people think I'm going to drown myself in a shower, for crying out loud? Look, all I want to do is take a shower. Nothing else. I'm fine. Really."

"I'm sorry, but it is hospital policy. There is nothing I can do about it." Mrs. Fogarty sat in a chair near the door.

Sam sighed as she bent her head in defeat. She was too tired to fight anymore. They were going to do what they wanted to her, no matter what she said. She went into the nearest stall and turned on the shower.

"How did everything get so messed up? All I wanted was for Brigid to see me, to know how I felt about her. To know that I loved her. Now I've ruined it all. I guess this is no less than what I deserve for what I have put her through," she whispered under her breath. She stepped under the spray and let the hot water wash over her. As she bathed, she realized how exhausted she was. "All I want to do now is sleep. Maybe when I wake up this whole nightmare will be over. I can use the time in here to rest. I don't have to do anything or talk to anybody. That's all I need."

After taking her vitals and weighing her, Mrs. Fogarty finally took Sam to her room. The nurse opened a heavy door and stood aside for Sam to enter. As Sam passed through the doorway, she noticed the door was steel with a window in the top half. The room was bare except for a mattress on a low frame, which looked bolted to the floor and the walls were covered in thick quilted padding. A small, but bright bulb in a ceiling lamp provided the light that kept shadows from forming in the corners.

"Oh, my God. I don't think I can do this. I can't do this. I need to get out of here."

"It's all right, Samantha," Mrs. Fogarty said. "It's only for tonight. This is part of the procedure set up by the hospital to protect you from doing any harm to yourself. I'll check on you through the night to make sure you're okay and we'll give you something to help you sleep. You won't even know you're in here until you wake up in the morning. Tomorrow we'll move you to a regular room. It will be okay, I promise."

Sam looked at the mattress and the walls again. Pulling on her inner strength, she took a deep breath. *I can do this.* "Okay."

"I'll be right back with your medicine." Mrs. Fogarty stepped out of the room, leaving her alone.

Sam jumped when she heard the lock on the door click shut. "Shit!" She realized she was locked in the room. She sat down on the mattress with her legs crossed under her. She put her hands over her face, feeling lost and alone. She sat like that until she heard a key turn in the door.

"I have something that should help you sleep through the night,"

Mrs. Fogarty said as she stepped into the room. "Take this."

She gave Sam two paper cups. One held a pill, while the other had some water. She swallowed the pill and washed it down. *Sleep. I don't even remember the last time I really slept.* Sam didn't wait for the nurse to leave before wrapping the covers around her.

Chapter Twenty-four

THE NEXT MORNING, JANET stepped out of the elevator carrying her bundle. She pressed the metal plate next to the door and held up her badge at the camera placed above the door and it wasn't long before she heard the buzzer. Janet pushed through the door into the psychiatric ward of the hospital.

"Hi, I'm here to see Samantha Bailey," Janet said as she held up her badge to the person at the nurses' station whom she didn't recognize. "Is she allowed visitors yet?"

"Hi, Janet. I'm Dr. Travis. I've seen you in the ER the few times I've been down there." The doctor held her hand out across the desk and Janet shook it. "Let me check her chart for you." Dr. Travis struck a few keys on the computer in front of her. "Nothing here says she can't have visitors. According to this, she has been withdrawn, so I don't know if she'll talk to you. Is she a patient of yours?"

"No, Samantha is a family friend. I came to check on her and bring her a few things to make her more comfortable. I also brought some reading material for her. Samantha's an avid reader, so I thought this would help fill some of her time."

"Since she's not your patient, there isn't much more I can share. She's in room 213."

"Thanks, Dr. Travis."

"No problem, Janet. Do us a favor, see if you can get her out of her shell. We can't do much up here if she is uncooperative."

"I'll see what I can do, Doctor. Hopefully, she'll talk to me."

Janet found Samantha's room and knocked on the door. She wasn't surprised when there was no answer. She took a deep breath and pushed through the door. Except for the light coming through the windows, the room was dark. Samantha was laying on the bed, curled up and facing away from the door. She had her legs pulled to her chest and the white hospital covers were wrapped tightly under her chin. Samantha looked like a small child, nothing like the vibrant person that had been at her house a couple of days earlier.

Janet sat on the edge of the bed and placed her hand gently on Samantha's back. Samantha didn't flinch. "Hi, Samantha, I brought you a few things I thought you would like. I stopped by your room and picked up some clothes for you. I also brought you some new books from Brigid's."

At the mention of her sister's name, Samantha's muscles tightened under Janet's hand.

"Brigid spent most of yesterday here. Brigid is worried about you, Samantha."

Samantha wiped her face with her pillowcase but didn't look up. Janet knew she was crying.

"She truly cares for you, Samantha. You have to believe that, especially now. I know it's hard being here, but the doctors and nurses will help you, but only if you let them." Janet paused a moment even as she kept rubbing Samantha's back. "Honey, I know you're scared right now, and maybe upset with yourself, but you have to get up. Nothing's going to get better by staying in bed hiding. These people can't help you unless you let them. Sweetie, what are we going to do with you? I can't let you lie here beating yourself up over this or being too afraid to do anything to help yourself.

"I want to tell you something. I don't want you to think I'm doing this just because I'm Brigid's sister. I'm here for you, Samantha. Brigid doesn't know that I've been in this situation before. When I was in high school, I had a friend named Gloria. We were best friends. After graduation, we went to different schools, but we stayed in touch over the years. About seven years ago she came home and moved in with her folks. I thought it was just until she got over her divorce. We didn't talk much though. Gloria seemed to want to distance herself and I let her. My life was busy with family, David, and work. Now I wish I hadn't allowed her to do that. I should have paid more attention. Maybe I would have noticed more.

"I was working when her parents brought her in to the ER one night, Gloria was in about the same shape as you were, if not worse. I watched as they restrained her. I asked her what was going on. Gloria looked at me as if I was some apparition and asked me to help her. When we parted, we were as close as sisters. It was the least I could do for her after so many years. I spent the next several months doing that. I supported her every step of the way the best I could.

"One of the reasons I helped her was my guilt for letting her push me away, but mostly it was trying to get Gloria back to the person I knew growing up. I want to help you find the person you were, Samantha, the person you are. You deserve that as much as anyone."

"She hates me," Samantha said with a sniffle.

"No, she doesn't, sweetie. She's a bit hurt and a little angry, but she doesn't hate you. I don't think she could ever hate you. I'm sure as soon as you start to feel better, she'll be in to see you."

Samantha stretched out and rolled over. "Do you really think Brigid will come? After what happened, do you really think she would want to talk to me?"

"I won't tell you it will be easy, Samantha, but I will tell you that I know in my heart that Brigid doesn't hate you. If you can get this under control, then I'm sure she'll be in to see you. And I'm sure she'll be willing to talk to you about what happened. Then you'll have a chance to explain everything to her and I'm sure Brigid will listen."

"I wish I could, Janet." Samantha turned her head away. "But I don't understand it myself. I don't know why I did the things I did. All I can say is that it made sense at the time. I just wanted her to know me, to be my friend. I figured the best way to do that was to be close to her. Any way I could. It's all so stupid."

Janet's heart broke for the woman. She knew that Samantha was at her most vulnerable. She gave Samantha a heartfelt hug. At first, Samantha tightened up, but, after a moment, she relaxed into the hug, crying. After a few minutes, she pulled away from Janet and wiped away her tears. She wiped her dripping nose on the sleeve of her hospital gown.

"I'm sorry about that," Samantha said weakly.

"Samantha, can I ask you a favor?"

"Sure. You're the only one who seems to care. What can I do for you?"

"Will you let your doctor talk to me about what is going on with you? That way, if you have any concerns or questions, I can help you. Would that be all right with you? And I know Brigid is concerned about you. It might help her understand things if I can explain it to her."

Samantha looked out the window for a long time before she answered. "Sure, I'll do that."

"It will be okay, Samantha. I promise. Just do what they tell you and you'll see. Things will get easier." Janet stood and placed a gentle kiss on the top of Samantha's head. "I'll check in with you after my shift is over, okay?"

"Sure, I'll be here," Samantha said in a low voice as Janet left the room.

***

Later that afternoon, Janet returned. The nurse on duty had called and told her Samantha wanted her to come upstairs.

"Hi, Beverly, they got you working hard?"

"Seems harder every day, Janet," Beverly said. "But I would rather be here than in the trenches of the ER. I get enough action for my taste here. What brings you up this way?"

"Samantha Bailey asked me to come up. Is she in her room?"

"No. She's in the conference room with the doctor, her duty nurse, and the social worker. They wanted to meet with Samantha and her family, and she asked for you. The room is down the hall on the right."

"Thank you." Janet turned and walked away. When she got to the room's closed entry, she took a deep breath and let it out slowly. She knew that what happened in there was going to decide Samantha's future. After a moment, Janet opened the door and stepped inside.

"Hi. I'm sorry I kept you all waiting."

"That's okay." A woman stood up and shook Janet's hand. "I'm glad you could make it. I'm Dr. Julia Winski, Samantha's psychiatrist."

"And I'm Samantha's primary nurse, Michele Blake." The nurse leaned over the table to also shake Janet's hand.

"Joseph Rosenthal is the head social worker up here and will be taking on Samantha's case," Dr. Winski said as she gestured at the man who sat next to Nurse Blake.

"Hi," Joseph said and made a slight wave.

"Now that we have the introductions out of the way, we can start. We like to go over these things with both the patient and family in one meeting so that we're all aware of the care the patient will need. I understand that Samantha has no family in the area, but she asked that you be included in this. I'm glad she has someone to support her."

Janet pulled up a seat next to Samantha. Samantha looked at her with a weak smile.

"You look a little better than this morning," Janet whispered although she thought Samantha looked scared to her core. Janet took one of Samantha's hands in her own. She gave it a reassuring squeeze, which Samantha returned, and let it go.

"So, Samantha, how are you feeling? I know some days can be tougher than others." Dr. Winski asked.

Samantha looked at Janet, who gave her a slight nod to reassure her. "Uhm, okay, I guess. I didn't sleep well last night, but I got up late this morning. Went and looked around a bit. The nurses had me have lunch with everyone else. That was okay, I guess. I can tell you I'm not crazy about the food here. And I met with Joe. We talked for a while. After that, I sat in my room reading. Oh, and I met with you for an hour."

"It's not a test, Samantha. You can relax. Take a deep breath," Janet said.

Samantha took a long inhale and let it out slowly.

"That's good, Samantha," Dr. Winski said. "I'd like to go over with you and Janet what we have concluded, based on what happened before you got here and what we have observed and talked about since then. Okay?"

"Okay. I think I'm ready to hear this."

"One of the things we talked about today was about what was going on with you before you got here. You remember the questionnaire I had you fill out?" Dr. Winski asked. Samantha nodded.

"Based on that, and the talks you and Joe had, we have agreed on a diagnosis for now."

Samantha clenched her fist tight. Janet placed her hand over it and squeezed it, hoping to give her some strength.

"It's a disorder known as Bi-Polar NOS," Dr. Winski said.

Samantha had a confused expression and a frown on her face. "I don't get it. What the hell is that supposed to mean?"

"Bi-polar disorder is more commonly known as manic-depression. You might know it that way. The NOS stands for Not Otherwise Specified. The disorder has two main types, one and two. Anything that doesn't fit those criteria we call NOS."

Samantha looked at Janet, who smiled at her. "I don't understand. I know I told you I get depressed a lot, but nothing like this ever happened before. How could I be manic? When did this happen?"

"Based on what you told me today, and what you told Dr. Winski, you have most likely had the disorder since early adulthood or as a teenager," Joe said.

"But I don't get it. You can't be right. I've never been like this before."

Dr. Winski went to the dry-erase board. She drew two horizontal parallel lines about an inch apart across the board.

"Samantha, this is the normal range of high and low emotions most people experience. It runs pretty steady. Manic depressive people have a completely different set of lines." She picked up a different color marker and drew a line from the bottom line down at an angle. "This would be how a person with bi-polar disorder feels during a low or depressive state."

Using a third color, she drew another line at an upward angle, from the new lower line to about three inches above the highest line.

"Then, instead of going back to the normal high range, they go past it. Sometimes by a little, but, more often than not, it is by a lot. Since, until recently, you've been able to function in a sort of routine fashion in your life, you most likely didn't go that high. Instead, you would be what we call hypo-manic, or the lesser line." Dr. Winski drew a line that went only about an inch above the top original line. "You probably barely noticed the highs, except for feeling really happy at times and full of energy. You might, at times, get a sense of being able to accomplish more tasks than usual."

Samantha nodded.

"The problem is that as these episodes occur, they become more frequent in period, longer in duration, and increase in strength. They can also be affected by stress. You told us that you had been under a great deal of stress at work before you came here."

"Yeah, but it wasn't any more than usual."

"Samantha, you yourself said that your last case was more difficult than the others and that you had reached your breaking point. Come on, Samantha, you can do this. I know you're strong enough," Janet said.

Samantha looked down for a minute or two, her brow furrowed. "Okay, supposing I have this bi-polar thing, what are you going to do to help me?"

"That is where all of us come in." Dr. Winski returned to the table and sat down. "I'll be prescribing you some medications. It may take us some time to find the right combination, but we'll get you there. We'll meet for a little while every other day during your stay here, and then later in my office. Joe will be in charge of your group and individual therapy."

"I'm a clinical social worker, so you will be seeing me every day, or sometimes twice a day," Joe said.

Michele will keep tabs on you during the day," Dr. Winski said. "Not to spy on you, but she will set up a schedule of activities and tasks for you to follow. We would like you to follow it since it's best for you to keep to a routine. It may be difficult at first, but please keep in mind that a set schedule will help you reduce your stress and insure you take your medications on time."

"How are you going to cure me? What treatment is there?"

"I'm sorry, Samantha, but there is no cure. This is a lifetime thing. But we can help you get stable. And, hopefully, with hard work, a day will come when this is a minor part of your life. That's about all I want to subject you to right now, Samantha. Do you have any other questions?" Dr. Winski asked.

"No, not really. I mean, I really don't understand all this." Samantha said.

"That's okay," Dr. Winski said. "It can be overwhelming at first. Why don't you and Janet go back to your room? Michele or Joe can answer any other questions you may have. If you need me, they can contact me and, if needed, I'll come back and talk to you."

"Okay."

"In the meantime, I am going to prescribe you some Lithium and Abilify and see how you do on them. We'll also give you something to help you sleep if you need it. The Lithium is a mood stabilizer and should even you out. The Abilify will help get rid of the noise that is bothering you and reduce your anxiety."

Dr. Winski stood up and the others followed suit. Janet took Samantha's elbow and walked her back to her room.

***

Janet returned to visit in the evening after her shift was over. She found Samantha sitting in a chair, more animated than she had been that morning and afternoon. She was working on one of the crossword puzzles books Janet had brought her.

"Hi, Samantha. How are you doing? You look better this evening."

"Hi, Janet! I'm doing a lot better. They gave me more of those medications they talked about. I even went to dinner with some people I met in group therapy. Some people here, it turns out, have the same thing I do. I get to go to therapy again with Joe tomorrow. In the meantime, I'm working on this." Samantha held up the book of crossword puzzles. "Oh, and I got a roommate. She seems nice enough but doesn't talk much. Seems she's in for depression. Mostly she just mopes around or lies on her bed. I think she's out watching the TV right now, otherwise I'd introduce you."

Janet sat on the bed opposite Samantha. She noticed Samantha's speech was moving fast. It concerned her a bit. She wasn't sure it was enough to mention to Samantha. *I'll have the nurses make a note for Dr. Winski when I leave.*

"I'm glad you're doing so well. I thought I'd stop by before I head home to see how you were settling in after this afternoon. I bought you some candy bars from downstairs." Janet handed over two bars. "That should hold you till morning. Just don't let the nurses see them."

Samantha winked as she took the candy from Janet. "Thanks. They have vending machines in the TV room, but I didn't have any money for it."

"In that case I'll bring you in some cash tomorrow. I know it's hard to survive on the small meals they serve in here."

"Thanks, Janet. You've been really great to help get me through this."

"Hey, it's no problem." Janet saw Samantha's eyes shine with unshed tears. "I want to help you deal with this. I have all the faith in the world that you can overcome it."

"Janet? Can I ask you some questions about everything?"

"Sure, sweetie, you can ask me anything. I'll answer them, if I can." Janet had expected this and had asked one of the social workers for some current literature on the disorder. The social worker gave her some pamphlets and articles on the subject, and she read them over her dinner break.

"How long will I have to be here? I mean, how long will the treatment last?"

"You won't have to stay here too long, Samantha, but the treatment is a lifetime thing. They can get you stabilized, but to stay that way you have to take your meds every day."

"Oh." Disappointment was apparent in her voice and in her eyes. "What will happen to me after I get out of here? How will I stay that way?"

"We'll get you a psychiatrist who will see you on a regular basis and help regulate and adjust your meds if needed. You should also get a good therapist, someone to talk to and help you cope with life a little better. This disorder has, and will continue to impact your life, Samantha. You have a lot of adjusting to do right now. I think that would help you a good deal in learning what your comfort zone is."

"My comfort zone?"

"Things like how to make your life less stressful, what might lead to an episode and how to handle one if it does happen, those kinds of things. Bi-polar is often aggravated by stress, so you need to learn how to reduce your stress levels and how to find out where your limits are."

"Okay, I can do all that. I think." Samantha's brows furrowed.

"I know you can, Samantha. I know you can."

"How long will I have to stay?"

"It depends, honey. They put you on some meds and they have to wait to see how you do on them. Once they see that you are pretty okay with it all they'll let you go home."

The word 'home' lingered between them.

"Home. I guess I don't really have one of those anymore, do I? I can't go back to Illinois. I don't have anything really significant there, and there is nothing I want there, not even memories. I had no true life. All I did was exist." Samantha sighed. "But I have no reason to stay here now either, do I? I gave up everything when I did all that to Brigid." Samantha's eyes shone again with tears that did not fall.

"No, you didn't, Samantha. You still have friends. I'll stand by you, and I know Brigid will too once she understands everything. She's just upset and confused right now. Just give her some time."

"Sure, Janet, okay." Samantha didn't sound the least bit convinced.

"Try and hang in there. It will get better. You just have to wait and see how tomorrow turns out. Stick to the schedule they put you on and you'll do okay."

"What's so important about this schedule that you and everybody keeps talking about, and how I have to keep it up? It sounds like I'm in the God-damn military."

"Samantha, honey, relax. Keeping to a routine is a way to help take away some of the day-to-day stress." Janet was caught off guard by the sudden change in Samantha's voice.

"Why couldn't they have told me that in the beginning? Why did I have to wait for you to clarify it? You would think people would want you to know this. All I ask for is a little God-damn consideration," she yelled.

"Calm down, Samantha." Janet spoke softly, hoping it would relax Samantha. "I'm sure somebody would have explained it in the morning."

"You're right. I'm sorry I blew up at you. It can be very frustrating here. That's the third time today I've lost my temper and I don't know why. I guess I'm a bit on edge."

"That's okay. I hate to do this to you, but David and the kids are waiting for me at home. I really should be going."

"That must be nice," Samantha said with longing, as her eyes stung holding back the tears from the overwhelming sense of loneliness she felt.

Janet laid her hand on Samantha's arm. "I'm sorry, Samantha. Really, I am. But I'll come by in the morning before my shift starts. It may be before visiting hours, so I can't promise anything."

"No, Janet, you can't. No one can," Samantha said in a quiet voice as she looked at the floor. "I'll be fine. You should go." She laid on the bed and rolled over with her back to Janet.

"I promise I'll see you tomorrow. You can count on it. I just don't know what time, okay?"

"Sure, that'll be fine."

Chapter Twenty-five

JANET WAS WORRIED. IT had been two days since anyone had seen Brigid and she wasn't answering her phone. Melissa said Brigid had called and asked if she could cover the store but wouldn't tell her for how long. Janet rang the doorbell and knocked on the door, but there was no answer.

"Great, I know you're in there, honey. I guess I'll just have to do it the other way." Janet took out her keys and unlocked and pushed open the door. "What kind of state am I going to find you in, Brigid? Samantha really needs you right now. I just hope you can be there for her."

All the lights in the house were off and, since most of the blinds were closed there was not much natural light either. Janet was surprised that Artemis wasn't at the door barking when she rang the doorbell and when she let herself in. There was no sign of Brigid.

"Brigid? Brigid?" Janet called as she walked from room to room. "Brigid, are you here?"

Artemis came in as if looking for her. The dog was not acting herself. Although her tail was wagging, she laid down in front of Janet instead of her usual jumping all over her. Janet went directly upstairs, Artemis pushed by and ran ahead, barking.

"Hey, girl, where's your mommy?" Janet asked the dog, her concern growing. Artemis looked toward Brigid's bedroom.

"Brigid, honey, it's Janet," Janet said as she opened the door. "Brigid, I'm coming in."

Janet's heart broke when she entered the bedroom. Brigid was curled under the covers with only her head sticking out and facing the window. The curtains were pulled slightly back allowing in some light.

Janet walked around the bed and found Brigid was sleeping. Her eyes were puffy, with dried tear tracks marring her face. Tissues were piled up in the trash pail next to the bed and a half empty box sat on the nightstand. Janet wondered when Brigid had showered last. *What am I going to do with you two? Samantha is barely willing to fight for her life, while you look like you're already giving up.*

"Brigid, honey, you have to get up," Janet said as she gently shook her sister by the shoulder. "Brigid, wake up. Come on, please."

Brigid stretched her legs and made an indistinguishable grunting sound, but not much else.

"God, I hope you're not drunk. Brigid, I need to talk to you. Get up!" Janet was losing her patience and used the tone she reserved for dragging the kids out of bed in the morning.

Brigid opened her eyes and looked up at Janet. "Janet, what do you want? Go away." She turned over and pulled the covers over her head.

"No. Get out of bed." Janet pulled the covers all the way down to the end of the bed.

"Hey!" Brigid protested. She sat up and tried to get the covers back. "What are you doing?"

"Getting your ass out of bed and into a shower. You look like crap. Come downstairs for something to eat after you bathe. I bet you haven't eaten anything in days. And then we talk. I have today off so don't think I'm leaving anytime soon."

Brigid stared at her sister. "What do you want from me, Janet?"

"I want you to get up and stop feeling sorry for yourself. You can't spend the rest of your life holed up here."

"Fine, I'll get up, but you can't make it any better. No one can." Brigid sounded defeated as she swung her feet to the floor.

"Come on. You'll feel better after you shower and eat." Janet watched Brigid as she walked to the bathroom. Once she closed the door behind her, Janet collected the trashcan and headed downstairs.

＊＊＊

An hour later Brigid finally made an appearance in the kitchen. Janet was relieved to see that she looked much better. Brigid's attitude was still bad, but at least she was clean. She had changed into a pair of well-worn and ragged jeans and an old t-shirt. Her hair was combed and pulled into a ponytail.

Janet pointed to one of the kitchen chairs. "Sit down. I made you some scrambled eggs and toast. There's tea on the table, help yourself." She turned back to the stove.

Like a scolded child, Brigid sat down and waited for her first meal in at least a day. Janet placed the food in front of her and, without a word, Brigid began eating, stopping only once to take a sip of tea. Neither of them spoke until she finished eating and the dirty plate was in the sink.

"Have you seen her?" Brigid asked, not looking up at her sister.

"Yeah, I've seen Samantha before and after my shifts. I'll go again once I leave here." Janet's spoke to her in the same tone she saved for her children when they were feeling sad.

"She's still in the hospital?"

"She'll be there for a few weeks." Janet watched for Brigid's reaction so she could figure out what was going through her head.

"Is it that serious?"

"It is, yeah."

"Will she be all right?" Brigid's eyes widened as her voice swelled with each question.

Janet didn't answer.

"Janet, will Sam be okay?"

Janet was relieved when Brigid referred to Samantha by name. "Ultimately, yeah, she'll be fine. It's going to be a long, difficult process getting there."

"What kind of process? What are they doing to her? Is it surgery?"

"No, not surgery." Janet assured her, reaching across the table and took her sister's hands in her own. She gave them a gentle, reassuring squeeze. "They are putting her on some medications that should help, but it may take a while before it works or until they find a good combination."

"What is it, Janet? What caused her to act the way she did? Is it a brain tumor? I've heard they can affect a person's behavior."

"It's nothing like that. Samantha had a sort of breakdown," Janet explained, looking her sister in the eyes.

"A breakdown?"

"Brigid, Samantha is suffering from a mental illness."

***

Now Brigid was confused. Sam was a little eccentric, but she always seemed so strong. Once she got to know people, she acted so self-assured. What her sister was saying made no sense to her. "What kind of mental illness?"

"Samantha's been diagnosed as Bi-polar, Brigid. She said I could talk to you about it."

"Bi-polar? I don't understand. What does that mean for Sam?" Brigid pulled her hands away.

"It means she has a long road ahead of her. The disorder affects her personality to some extent. She has been through a gamut of emotions for some time, maybe her whole adult life, with each episode more extreme than the last one."

"And that means what?"

"It means that Sam hasn't been in control of herself, or her emotions for some time. She goes from feelings of euphoria to deep depression. She can begin getting a handle on it once her new medications kick in. In the long run the doctors hope to stabilize her, to get her emotions to remain normal." Janet explained everything Dr. Winski had told them in the meeting.

"Oh, my God. Poor Sam. What is she going through? How is she now?"

"Scared mostly and feeling alone. She had a setback yesterday. One of the medications they put her on, Lithium, made her manic symptoms worse, so they started her on a new drug last night. Hopefully it will help."

Brigid's forehead was wrinkled with worry lines.

"Once she is stable, she'll be back to herself," Janet said.

"Being herself." Brigid repeated in a soft voice. "What does that mean, Janet? If she was sick with this the whole time, I've known her, do I understand anything about who she is? Maybe the stalker is who she truly is. How can I be sure the person I fell in love with is still there? Wow that is the first time I've said that out loud to anyone, even to myself."

Janet nodded. "I know, it's hard to come to terms with that, Brigid. Especially after Tina."

"You said this is a personality disorder. So, it changes her personality. When she takes the medications, it will alter who she is now, won't it?"

"Yes. No..." Janet struggled find the right answer. "It will change some parts of her, but it won't change the core of who she is."

"She'll still be the same outgoing, funny person she was before the other day? Or will she be the person we saw in that motel room and who stalked me for weeks?" Brigid knew she was backing her sister into a corner, but she didn't care. She wanted answers—ones she could deal with.

"Honey, she is still Samantha. She always will be. Some parts of her personality will be more stable than before. Most of her odd behavior will go away. But deep down she won't change. She will continue to be the gentle, strong, and caring person you came to love."

"But what if she's not?"

"I don't know what to tell you, Brigid. I really don't."

"How can we be sure of who she is?"

"I didn't know Samantha before. I didn't know her until I met her at the house, But I've gotten to know her now and I can tell you that she is a tough person. She can work through this. I know she can. She has shown the courage to face this and the determination not to let it beat her. That hasn't changed. I don't think that kind of thing can be affected by her disorder. She is still the same person."

"I want to believe you, Janet."

"The only changes will be for the better, Brigid, for each of you in your own way. It can bring you closer together. Show you who you are deep inside. And she can be your whole world, Brigid. You have to see that."

"What do you want me to say, Janet? That everything is fine? That none of this matters? Well, I can't, because it does." Brigid's voice rose until she was shouting. "You're telling me the person I knew may or may not come out of that hospital. That the person I love may no longer exist." A waterfall of tears spilled onto her cheeks and quickly turned to miserable sobs.

Janet went to Brigid and pulled her into her arms. Brigid buried her face into Janet's chest as Janet held her, rocking back and forth.

"Sweetie, that is not what I'm saying to you at all. Samantha is still Samantha. That will never change. You have to listen and believe. Some of her more eccentric or strange behaviors will go away. Samantha may not be as outgoing, but she'll still be the identical person; the person that you love."

Brigid tried to calm herself after a few moments. She grabbed a napkin off the table and swiped impatiently at her tear streaked face and runny nose. She took several deep breaths until only a few errant tears remained.

"But can I love Sam the way she will be?" she asked, glad to be able to share with her sister how she felt about Sam, or at least the Sam she knew before all the insanity began.

"Only you can decide that, Brigid. If your love is strong enough, and I trust in my heart that it is, then the minor changes won't make a difference. I believe you can do it. Talk to her, Brigid. Go see for yourself who she is. That's the only way to know for sure."

"I don't know if I can. I'm not sure my heart could take it right now if I discovered she's no longer the person I found. When she came into The Wordsmith, it was as if she discovered herself. Can you tell me if that happens again, will it be someone entirely different?"

"It could happen, Brigid, I won't lie to you. But give her the chance to show you who she is now. I think you'll still love her no matter what you find. But no matter what, I don't believe you will see the person who was in that motel room. You will see a scared, lonely individual who wants your forgiveness and to have the opportunity to love you back."

Brigid sat and looked at a spot on the table. Janet went to the sink and began rinsing the dishes. Brigid's forehead furrowed as she picked at the spot on the table.

"Okay, I'll go see her," Brigid finally said in a firm, quiet voice.

"That's great. You can go with me this afternoon." Janet rejoined her at the table.

"I don't know that I'm ready to just yet," Brigid said, holding one hand up. "I have a lot to get used to before I see her. Maybe in a day or two."

"Okay, whenever you're ready, we'll go. Can I tell Samantha you'll come? I think it would help her right now. Give her something to focus on and look forward to."

Brigid waited a moment before answering. "Sure, you can tell her. I don't know what good it will do, since I can't say what'll happen when I do go."

"Simply knowing that you are coming and willing to talk to her will help."

"All right, whatever you think. I really don't like the idea of Sam being locked up in that place."

"She's not really locked up, Brigid. She's been there long enough that she can check herself out anytime. And she can go outside every day. Samantha has come to realize the hospital is the best place for her right now. It's a good environment for her. There is little she has to worry about now, so the hospital is a safe place for her. She can relax and not feel any pressure or stress. She is able to get used to being herself before she has to deal with the real world again, and it gives the meds a chance to start working. It truly is the perfect spot for her. Honest."

"If you say so, Janet, but you said she was scared. What is she scared of?"

"I think she is afraid of what you think of her because of what she did and what her diagnosis is."

"Well, I can't reassure her about any of those things. At least not yet." Brigid was sorry she couldn't give Janet or Sam, a better answer.

"Knowing that you're willing to talk to her should take away some of her fears."

Brigid got up and stood in front of the sink. She looked out the window, past the yard and out into the woods. She realized that Samantha had spent a lot of time there, watching her from some secret spot. The idea of being watched still made the hairs on the back of her neck stand up.

"If you don't mind, Janet, I'm going to go outside for a while. I have a lot to think about right now and I want to do it alone," she said without turning around.

"Sure, Brigid. I'll call you later and see how you're doing. I'm going to go see Samantha now."

"You can tell her I'll be by...I just don't know when." Brigid turned to face her sister. "I can't promise anything to either of you, not yet at least. I wish I could, I really do."

"I understand. It's a lot to take in right now." Janet gave her sister a comforting hug and kissed the top of her head. "I'll explain it to her. Don't worry."

Brigid turned and looked back out the window as Janet left. After a few moments she called Artemis. The dog came running, with her tail wagging furiously. Brigid opened the sliding glass door and stepped outside. Artemis went scampering out before her and made a beeline for the woods. Brigid heard her barking and running around among the trees. Within a few minutes, Artemis came back out and looked around, as if she was confused. She looked at Brigid and then back at the woods. After a moment she rejoined Brigid and began whimpering.

Brigid realized Artemis was looking for Sam. She looked at where Artemis had been looking. "Hmm. It's definitely at the right angle for the pictures." She pondered the new information. Artemis sat beside her and Brigid mindlessly ran her fingers through her soft fur.

"Girl, you're usually so guarded when it comes to strangers. Why did you accept Sam so easily? Do you sense something in Sam, something that makes you think she's not a threat? God. Why does it seem everyone thinks Sam is fine but me? Is there something I'm not seeing? Maybe I should give her a second chance? I'm so unsure about what to do. When I look back on it with hindsight, nothing she did was really threatening." She looked at the spot where she suspected Sam took the pictures from. "Or am I just thinking that because I want it to be true?"

She was only vaguely aware of Artemis running off before she came back with a ball and placed it in her lap. Brigid threw it as she continued trying to decide what to do. For the rest of the late morning and early afternoon she played with Artemis and thought about the whole situation. The only conclusion she could come up with was that she needed to talk to Sam.

Chapter Twenty-six

SAM PACED THE HALLS of the ward. She had finished all the puzzles Janet had given her, as well as many of the books. Nothing was on her schedule and she didn't feel like sitting down. Something inside wanted to move—the constant motion was a comfort to her. It was the exact feeling she had when she walked the streets. Sam looked up and saw her nurse coming toward her with a concerned look on her face, which made Samantha feel even more nervous.

"Samantha, will you come with me? We need to talk for a few minutes."

What did I do? I haven't missed anything on my schedule. Maybe there's something else wrong.

"Let's go inside and talk," Michele said as she led Sam back to her room.

Sam sat on the bed, leaving Michele the chair.

"Samantha, I'm a little concerned about some of your behavior. You seem restless today. How are you feeling?"

"Okay, I guess. I just feel like moving around. I finished the puzzles and most of the books Janet gave me. I think being cooped up in here is starting to get to me."

"You've read all the books and finished the puzzles she gave you? I thought those would keep you busy for weeks."

"Yeah, I finished them all. Wasn't I supposed to?"

"I think that was a pretty big pile to go through. I would think the crossword puzzles alone would take a day or two, Are you still hearing things?"

Sam didn't want to answer the question, so she kept quiet.

"Samantha?"

"Maybe. I don't know. I've heard some music the last few nights before I went to bed. Is it possible someone had a radio on?"

"No one on the floor near you has a radio. I'm sorry, Samantha, but the only logical answer has to be that you're having auditory hallucinations. How are you thinking? Are you able to focus well or are your thoughts racing?"

"My mind does seem to be acting on overdrive sometimes. It's like my brain feels the need to constantly be doing something. It just doesn't know what." Sam felt as if she had failed somehow. "I am able to focus well though, I think." She looked Michele in the eyes. She was glad she could answer one of the questions in what she thought was the right way.

"That's good. How focused are you?"

"Well, I read a whole book yesterday."

"How big was the book?"

"Uhhmm, I think it was about three-hundred pages or so."

"That's an awful lot to read in one day. Have you done it before?"

"Yeah. Ever since I got to town I've been reading like that."

"What about before then?"

"No, not really. I read quite a bit, but not as much as now."

"Okay, Samantha. I'm going to mention this to Dr. Winski. I think you're still a little on the manic side, so I'd like to see if we can increase the dosage on some of the meds. Maybe we can switch you to something else."

Sam slumped her shoulders in self-pity.

"Don't worry, Samantha. I know it feels like it's a step back, but we'll get you settled soon."

"All right, Michele, whatever you say, I'll take your word for it." She doubted every word of it. She had let everyone down, including Brigid, the only person who mattered. As the door closed behind Michele, Sam buried her head in her pillow and cried in frustration. After a moment she threw the pillow across the room.

"Fuck! I thought I was doing so much better. Now I'm back at square one. It's never going to be better. How can I offer Brigid anything?" Sam picked the water pitcher off the table and hurled it against the wall, watching as the water sprayed everywhere.

One of the nurse's aides opened the door. "Is everything okay in here?"

"Everything is fucking great," Sam turned away from the woman.

Chapter Twenty-seven

BRIGID STOOD IN THE hallway outside the entry door to the psychiatric ward. She showed up at the hospital as visiting hours were starting but stayed downstairs until she worked up the courage to even approach the visitor's desk. After the staff okayed her visit, she took the elevator upstairs. Now she was once again trying to find strength to open the door and face Sam.

What do I say to her? 'Hi, how are you?' God that is stupid. Maybe I should simply be honest with her. Tell her about why I'm here. But, why am I here? Do I even know? Maybe I should go home and work this all out ahead of time. As she was about to turn and leave, a woman rushed up to her.

"Excuse me?" the nurse said as she put her hand on Brigid's arm. "Are you Brigid?"

"Yes," she said.

"Great. I'm Michele. I'm Samantha's primary nurse. Janet said you might be stopping by. She described you to me just in case you did. This way I could show you to Samantha."

"Oh. I was here to see her, but I think it's not such a good idea after all. I'm going to go home and try again tomorrow. How is Sam doing?"

"She's mostly stable."

Brigid waited for more of an explanation, but none came. "Other than that, how is she? Has she settled in okay? Is she taking everything well?"

"I'm sorry, I can't tell you that. You'll have to ask Samantha those questions," Michele said as she swiped her card and unlocked the doors. She motioned for Brigid to follow her. "She's not in there right now but she should be here in a moment."

Brigid looked over the nurse's shoulder and saw Sam coming down the hall. Her head was bent, and her shoulders slumped. As Brigid watched her, Sam looked up and stopped walking. Their eyes locked. Brigid felt her heart skip. She took a deep breath to relieve the tightness she felt in her chest as she looked into Samantha's eyes. Sam looked drawn and her eyes didn't sparkle the way they used to.

"I'll leave you two to catch up," Michele said as she turned and made her way back to the nurses' station. "Samantha, why don't you two sit over in the visiting area. It's empty for now."

* * *

Sam shook herself out of her daze and began walking toward Brigid. *I'm sure she hates me. I'll let her have her say and let her go. It's for the best, she thought.* Sam smiled at Brigid. "Hi. How are you? I can't believe you came. What are you here for? If it's to tell me to go to hell, I understand."

"Hi, I, uhm, came by to see how you were," Brigid said. "Janet told me you could use some visitors. I brought you some books."

Sam thought it strange that Brigid was so nervous. Sam expected nothing but anger. She had been prepared for that. But now, Brigid had her confused. "Sure, uh, let's go sit down? There's, uhm, no one in there." Sam waved toward the sitting area.

Brigid followed Sam.

"Uh…" Sam realized she was about to repeat herself and stopped before she did. She covered her slight stutter by clearing her throat. "Why don't you have a seat?" She pointed to the one of the chairs in the room as she sat on the one across from it and began picking at the loose threads of the cushion.

* * *

Brigid sat in the chair next to the window. The sunshine coming through the window made the room cheerier than she expected it would be. She had expected white antiseptic walls and cold impersonal furnishings. While the room was sparse, what was there gave Brigid a warm feeling. The wall was covered by a scenic mural Brigid recognized as the town's riverfront. She moved her foot and hit the bag next to it.

"Oh, yeah, I brought you some books to read. I figured you'd be a little bored if you ran out." Brigid held up her package.

"Thanks." Sam accepted the bag and peeked inside with a look of pleasure on her face.

"Janet said you had finished the ones she brought you, so I picked several long ones to help keep you busy." Brigid put her hands in her coat's pockets. She began to play with her car keys as her nervousness

130

overcame her. "I know you'd feel crazy without them." Brigid looked up, her eyes wide. "Oh my God, I didn't mean it to sound like that. Of course, I don't think that would make you worse. At least I assume it won't."

"It's okay, I know what you meant. No offense taken. So, what did you bring me?"

"Look them over and tell me if you've already read them or would rather have something else. I can get you others if you want."

"No, these will be fine. I'm sure I'll love them."

Both women glanced at each other, though neither one could look at the other for too long. Brigid looked down. Sam looked up at that moment and watched Brigid. She admired how Brigid's hair appeared mahogany in the sunlight.

"You're so beautiful," Sam said in the barest whisper. Sam hoped Brigid hadn't heard her, but an awkward silence followed. "I wanted to say to you..."

"I came by to tell you..." Brigid said at the same time.

"You go first," they said simultaneously

They laughed a little, breaking away some of the tension.

"You go ahead," Brigid finally said.

Sam lost a bit of her nerve and looked away. *I can't think when I look in those eyes.* She looked down. "I wanted to say how sorry I am for everything I did to you. You didn't deserve any of it." She sighed. "I'll understand if you hate me. The things I put you through these last few weeks were unacceptable. I'm surprised you want to see me."

"Sam, look at me."

Sam looked up into Brigid's deep chocolate eyes.

"Why did you do it? Why were you stalking me?"

Sam took a deep breath and let it out in a long sigh. "I don't know how to explain it to you. How do you explain such insanity? But you deserve an explanation, I know. I saw you in town and at the bookstore. You were so nice to me that first day that I had to get to know you. I wanted to know everything about you. Who you were, what you were like. I didn't know what to do. My thinking was so messed up. It seemed obvious that the best way to know you was to see you, to follow you, and see what you did."

She paused and looked down as she picked at the seat cushion. "After watching you, I knew I wanted to know you and for you to know me, to see me. And you did. You were the only one in town who saw me and took the time to talk to me. You showed me the kind of person you are, so I started sending you the notes. I figured that was the best way to show you how I was feeling. I thought you would understand."

"But why the pictures, Sam? Why did you take them and send them to me?"

"I wanted you to see yourself the way I did. You're beautiful, both inside and out. When you play with Tyler and Deidra or Artemis, you are so alive. You aren't the reserved image you portray to everyone. I saw in you someone who loves life, and I wanted to be a part of it any way I could. Because you are such a beautiful person, both in your physical being and your spiritual one." She took a breath. "Because I fell in love with you." Sam waited for the rejection she was sure would come next.

Brigid was stunned. "You love me? You did all of this because you love me? What kind of person does that, Sam?"

Sam looked out the window without answering.

Brigid thought about it for a moment. The wandering, the notes, the photos, Sam's actions at the store and with Brigid's family. It dawned on Brigid who would do that. Brigid looked up and saw that Sam was still looking out the window. "Someone who isn't thinking clearly."

"What did you say?"

"I said 'someone who isn't thinking clearly.' I think I understand, Sam. Only a person who is in the throes of a mental illness would do what you did."

"Well, I don't know that I was in the 'throes.'"

"Janet tried to tell me. She explained about the obsessive behavior and the euphoria. When I think of the poems you chose, I can see that now. You picked the poems that reflected your moods."

"I'm sorry."

"No, Sam. There's nothing to be sorry for, not anymore, not for this. I can't hold something you had no control over against you. You're being strong and brave by getting help. I believe that you will get well and be the person you were."

They sat in silence for a moment.

"I forgive you, Sam." Brigid took a deep breath and looked into Sam's eyes and saw the sparkle of tears. Sam seemed to be shocked that Brigid was willing to forgive her. Brigid's heart broke. She couldn't take it anymore and her tears began to fall. "I love you, too. I don't know when it happened or why, but somewhere along the way, Sam, I fell in love with you. But I don't know where to go from here."

***

Sam looked up. The tears fell for the love she lost, the love she threw away. "I don't deserve the love of someone as kind and gentle as you, Brigid, a person who can offer forgiveness to someone like me after everything I did. I'm sorry, Brigid. I know I've ruined any chance with you. That you forgive me is more than I can expect from anyone."

"I'm sorry, Sam. I don't know what else to tell you. I'm very confused right now. I don't know what to do, or how I feel. I did love you, but I don't know if I can still love you. So much has changed. You have changed

"But I haven't changed, Brigid. I am still the same person I was. The doctor said I would be more stable, steadier, my thinking clearer. But underneath it all I am still me."

***

Brigid looked into Sam's eyes. What she saw there took her breath away. She could see Sam in those eyes, see her soul. As if Sam was opening a window for Brigid to peer through. And the soul she saw was Sam's—the Sam she fell in love with.

"I think I can still love you. But I'm still hurt by what you did. I trusted you and you took advantage of that. I offered you friendship and you used that to get closer to me, to get what you wanted with no seeming consideration for how it would make me feel. But I still believe in hope. If you can get well, maybe we can start over. Begin again and maybe we can get our feelings back or create new ones."

"You have a beautiful soul, Brigid. Only someone like you would forgive me and give us a second chance. If I can do anything to help you love me again, I will do it. I swear to you that there will never be a reason to feel betrayed again. I can make this right, Brigid, I can feel it. Can you?"

Brigid looked at her, looking for any sign of the insanity she had witnessed before. She found none. But her soul reached into Sam's eyes and felt at home. This was where she was meant to be, she admitted to herself.

"I feel it. I feel you want it as much as I do, Sam. But is it enough?" Brigid's doubts surfacing again.

"If we take it slow and work on it together, I believe it is. Let me have enough faith for both of us, please? I know I can do this."

"Yes, Sam, let's take it slow. Maybe we can find what we lost."

"I promise we will, Brigid." Sam stood up and pulled Brigid up with her. Sam lowered her head, and when her lips were a mere hair's breath away, she stopped. But Brigid suspected Sam was letting her decide what happened next. Brigid allowed Sam to continue. When their lips met, she felt her essence soar. It was like coming home after being lost at sea.

Sam's gentle kiss was full of promises of what the future held. Brigid wrapped her arms around Sam, balling her shirt in her fists. Sam ran the tip of her tongue along Brigid's lips. When she felt the gentle caress of Sam's tongue against her own, she let out a deep moan and all felt right with them again.

***

Sam was overcome by the emotion of being granted a second chance. She pulled Brigid closer to her and ran her fingers through Brigid's soft hair. Sam wanted to memorize the feel of it. She never wanted to let this woman out of her arms again. For the first time in her life, she knew what love and home were.

She couldn't stand the raw emotion of it all and pulled away. "I love you, Brigid Fitzpatrick," she said as she looked into Brigid's eyes.

"I love you too, Samantha Bailey."

Chapter Twenty-eight

SAM LAY IN HER room at Janet's house. She had been staying there since she left the hospital a week ago. The stay in the hospital had been the longest thirty days in her life. Brigid stopped by for regular visits, but there was no repeat of the kiss. Sam was too unsure of herself to press forward, but now that she was at Janet's, she started to think of a future with Brigid.

The living arrangements worked fine until the kids had a fighting match and became loud and whiney. For some reason it made Sam irritated and shaky. She tried to shut out the stress and hide in her room with the lights off. She didn't know what was wrong or what to do but being in the dark helped with the little bit of quiet she gained.

She appreciated Janet making the offer to stay with her and her family during the last few days Sam was in the hospital. Sam tried to tell her that she would be fine at the motel, but Janet insisted that Sam needed someone to look after her while she made the transition back into her normal life. Sam didn't want to admit it, but she was more than a little scared about leaving the hospital. She expected a whole new world to be out there, one she was not prepared to deal with anymore.

But now she lay in the dark in Janet's guest room, on the verge of tears, and she had no idea why. The noise had quieted down, but it didn't relieve as much of the stress as Sam needed. *I just need it all to go away.* The door opened, allowing a stream of light onto the bed. Sam turned her head away as if the light hurt.

"Samantha? Are you all right, sweetie?" Janet asked as she moved into the room and sat on the edge of the bed. She put a hand on Sam's back and rubbed it as she often did when her children were upset. Sam flinched under her touch. "Honey, what's the matter? Do you want to tell me?"

"No," Sam buried her head deeper into her pillow and pulling away from Janet's gentle touch, "I'm fine, just leave me alone."

Janet went to the medicine cabinet and looked at the bottles, picking one out. She poured two tablets in her palm and got a bottle of water from the box on top of the dresser.

"Here, Samantha. Take these. They'll help, I promise." Janet held the pills out for Sam.

Sam didn't move for a few moments before she rolled over and took the pills and water. When she finished, she turned back over.

Janet sat in the armchair, leaving the door slightly ajar while she watched over Sam.

"Janet, can you close the door please? The light is bothering me."

"Sure, hun. We'll talk about this tomorrow."

Sam didn't say anything as she lay on her bed trying to avoid the light. She felt Janet sitting on the bed next to her.

Janet stayed until Sam relaxed into light doze. "We can't ignore this, as much as you want to." Sam heard her say as she closed the door behind her.

***

Sam woke up feeling groggy. It was how she felt most days now. She didn't have to look at the clock to know it was after ten. Since she was put on the meds in the hospital, she didn't wake before ten or eleven. Samantha spent several moments fighting the urge to go back to sleep. Once Janet left for work, there was no one around to wake her up, and the temptation to sleep was powerful. But she knew she needed to get up to stay on her routine.

Sam rolled out of bed, nearly landing face down on the floor. Standing on unsteady legs, she walked over to the medicine cabinet. Pulling out three bottles, she began picking one of each pill. She washed them down with some water and left her room in search of breakfast. She walked into the kitchen and headed for the teakettle, hoping the caffeine would help her wake up. On top of the pot was a note from Janet.

"Samantha, please call your doctor about yesterday. I think she should know about it."

"Janet's right, but I hate to call. What if she's busy? What if she thinks I'm overreacting? I don't want to be a pest or annoy her. I see her every three days anyway," Sam said to the empty kitchen. "But if I don't call Janet will know."

Sam thought about it several minutes and decided she had no choice but to make the call. "Whatever that was last night was too scary to let happen again. I have to get a handle on this if I expect a future with Brigid." *Maybe I should go see Brigid.* She shook her head and decided waiting another day or two would be best. Maybe once she was feeling better, she would stop into the store.

Since Sam got out of the hospital, they hadn't seen each other. Brigid visited her while she was still in the hospital and they had talked about the possibility of a future together, but since being released, Sam had limited their visits. Samantha was keeping her distance. She felt too insecure in her new life to offer Brigid anything. She sighed and picked up the phone.

"Hello, Dr. Winski's office. How can I help you?"

"Hi, this is Samantha Bailey. I need to talk to Dr. Winski, or better yet leave her a message if I could."

"I can take a message. Is this an emergency?"

"No, I just want to let her know I had a bit of an episode last night. I figured she'd want to know about it."

"Sure, can you hold on a minute?"

"Yeah, fine." Sam waited several minutes before the receptionist came back on the line.

"The doctor would like to see you this afternoon. Are you available at two o'clock?"

"I suppose." Sam hated that the doctor thought it important enough for her to come in a day early.

"Fine, we'll see you at two then," the receptionist said.

"Okay."

***

Sam was uncomfortable as she sat in the psychiatrist's waiting room. She wasn't used to the atmosphere of a psychiatrist's office. The room was full, each person with his or her own problems. No one made eye contact, yet she felt like everyone was looking at each other.

Finally, the door opened and Dr. Winski called her in. Dr. Winski had a small outside practice and Sam was lucky the doctor was able to take her as an outpatient. Once she was in the office, Sam sat on the couch. It was cliché but comfortable. The warm brown tones of the office were inviting, and the desk was cluttered with files and pictures Sam assumed were photos of the doctor's children.

Sam crossed her legs and waited while Dr. Winski sat at her desk and examined her file.

"What happened, Samantha?"

"Uh, I don't know what happened. It seemed like everything was fine and then, all a sudden, it wasn't."

"Can you tell me how you felt?"

"Well, irritated mostly. Then I started shaking. I felt fine one minute and uncontrollable anger the next. All I wanted was a dark quiet place to calm down, so I hid in my room."

Dr. Winski scrawled notes in Sam's file. "How did you feel physically?"

"My heart was racing and my whole body was shuddering from trying to control myself."

"And how do you feel now?"

"Better. The irritation is gone, and I don't feel so much like I want to hide."

"Are you still feeling agitated, like you want to jump out of your skin, or restless?" Dr. Winski looked at her as she asked the question.

"Maybe a little," Sam said after thinking about it for a few moments.

"You haven't stopped jiggling your leg since you sat down." Dr. Winski pointed at the offending leg with her pen "Have you been doing that a lot today?"

Sam looked at her legs and realized that she was, in fact, shaking one. Her foot was in constant motion, making little circles in the air. She hadn't realized it until now. "I think so. I'm not sure. I've felt like I need to be doing something all the time. I cleaned the house and did the laundry and dishes this morning, and then I watched television. But now that I think about it, I was doing it while I was on the sofa. Damn! I thought I was being productive for once in a long time."

"Well, I think we both know what is happening—"

"Yeah, I'm manic again, aren't I?"

"Yes, I think so. Do you have any idea what might have set it off?"

"No, I don't think so. I was hanging out with Janet and the kids when I began to not feel well. The kids were arguing about something and I was trying to watch television. Suddenly, the irritation set in. When I felt like I couldn't take it anymore, I left."

"What couldn't you take?"

"The arguing. It was loud and chaotic. I just couldn't handle it." Sam remembered how out of control and scared she had been.

"Here is what I would like you to do," Dr. Winski said. "I want you to increase the dosage on two of your medications. We can increase the mood stabilizer to 200 mg and the anti-psychotic to 15 mg. I think for now we can leave the anti-depressant where it is. I may change you to a different anti-depressant in the future, but for now let's leave it. How are you sleeping?"

"Not so well. I have a lot of trouble shutting my mind down to sleep. The slightest noise wakes me up, but then I can't seem to wake up in the morning."

"I can prescribe something that should help you fall asleep a little better and let you sleep through the night."

"Thanks. That will help a lot. I think I get off balance when I don't get enough sleep."

"All right, here are your new prescriptions. I'd like to see you again in two days." Dr. Winski handed Sam copies of the prescriptions. This will be sent to the pharmacy you're using so you just need to pick them up. They should be ready by the time you get there.

"Fine, I can do that."

"Did you find a therapist yet?"

"I have an appointment tomorrow with someone you recommended."

"Good. You can tell me how it goes the next time I see you."

As Sam left the office, she glanced at the prescriptions in her hand. After all the sessions, drugs, and therapy, Sam hoped that something, anything would work.

Chapter Twenty-nine

BRIGID STOOD AT THE counter ringing up customers. So far, she had given wrong change three times and rung up the incorrect amount twice, among other mistakes. Her mind wasn't on her work and it showed.

Brigid wondered why she hadn't heard from Sam much since she left the hospital. Brigid had called her at Janet's house several times, but their conversations were awkward, almost stiff. She got the sense that Sam didn't want to talk to her. The one-time Brigid went to the house, Sam had begged off, claiming she was tired and needed to lie down. Janet tried to explain that some of Sam's medications made her tired for a good part of the day. But Brigid felt like she was being pushed away. *I don't understand why she won't talk to or see me. After we kissed, I thought everything was worked out.*

Melissa cleared her throat next to her. Brigid jumped and dropped the shopping bag of books she was holding.

"Do you want to keep those books, or hand them to the customer?" Melissa asked.

The customer was staring at Brigid with a curious look on her face. Brigid handed them to the customer who turned and left.

"Okay. The store is empty, so I'm going to ask, what is with you today?" Melissa said. "I've never seen you this distracted before."

"It's nothing," Brigid said. "I have a few things on my mind."

"Those things wouldn't involve Samantha, would they? I haven't seen her around. Are things okay with you guys?"

"I think so. I haven't had a chance to talk to her lately."

"Are you still mad at her?" Melissa asked. Brigid had filled her in about Sam stalking her but had assured her all was forgiven. "I mean for what she did to you? That was a big deal. I don't know that I could forgive someone for doing that to me."

"No, I'm not mad about that. At least I don't think I am. But her not talking to me is making me angry all over again. I don't know if I'm upset with her for what she did, or at the situation and the fact that I can't see her. It feels like she's trying to get out of being with me. The frustrating part is that, without talking to her, I don't know how to fix things."

"Well. Why don't you call her? See if she wants to go out or something. That would give you guys a chance to talk."

"I don't know. It feels like she's pushing me away. Maybe she just said what she did to get me to forgive her. What if she didn't really mean any of it? How can I be sure I didn't forgive her too soon? Could she have changed so much that she would lie to me?"

"Are you sorry you forgave her, Brigid?"

"I'm not sure about anything anymore. What if I shouldn't have forgiven her? Do you think she was really sorry?"

"I don't know. Only you and Samantha can know that for certain. Why don't you call and talk to her?"

"I'm not sure I want to. What if she says it was all just a ploy? I think it would be too devastating at this point."

"How about we put it up to chance?"

"What do you mean?"

"I know you. You're trying to decide what to do. So, here's the deal. You mess up with one more customer you have to call her. Invite her over for dinner or something and you guys talk it over. Get some answers, since you obviously need them."

"You're betting me?" Brigid lifted eyebrow. "You want me to bet on my life?"

"Sure, why not? Brigid, you have nothing to lose. If you win, you don't have to do anything you don't want to do. But if you lose, you have to call her today and set something up. You have the opportunity to know one way or the other."

"You're crazy!"

"Why? What does it matter? Your only choice is to talk to Samantha if you want to learn the truth. One way you do it now and get it over with, the other way you wait and struggle to decide what to do and maybe you choose to do nothing, in which case you will never have any answers." Melissa raised her arms and shrugged. "I know you, Brigid. You want to make the right decision. This way you take the burden off yourself."

"Okay, fine, I'll do it, but I still think this is stupid."

For the next several hours, the women worked together, stacking books, ringing up customers, and helping people find what they needed. Brigid made a conscious effort to avoid any slipups. It wasn't long before her mind drifted to random thoughts and memories, which led to thinking about Samantha again. After totaling an order on the cash register, Brigid handed the change to the gentleman. He looked at his hand and then back at Brigid.

"Miss, I gave you a twenty."

"Oh, yes, you did, I'm sorry." Brigid handed him a five-dollar bill. "Here you go. This should be right."

Brigid started back to the information desk, but Melissa blocked her path, holding out the cordless phone.

"Call."

"Call what?"

"Call Samantha. You lost the bet, so here." Melissa put the phone in Brigid's hands and shuffled her into the back room for privacy.

"You want me to call her now?"

"No time like the present, and this way you have no chance to back out. So, call."

"Fine.

Brigid dialed the number for Janet's house. She expected no one to answer and was surprised when there was a voice at the other end.

"Hello?" Sam said.

Brigid was amazed at the sensations that ran through her as she heard that one word. Her body calmed down, replaced by a soothing tingling sensation, and her confidence returned. "Hi, Sam; it's Brigid."

"Hi. Nobody's home if you're looking for Janet. I'll tell them you called."

"No, I called for you," Brigid said in a rush, hoping to keep Sam on the line. "Uh, I wanted to talk to you."

"Oh." Sam sounded resigned.

"I called to see if I could interest you in dinner tomorrow night."

"Dinner? I'm not sure I'm up for that right now, Brigid."

"Please, Sam. We really need to talk. I won't take no for an answer this time. I really need to see you."

"I don't know—"

"No, Sam, you can't keep avoiding me. For both our sakes, just talk to me."

"You were right. You're not going to take no for an answer, are you?"

"No, most certainly not."

"Okay, what time should I be there?"

"Six-thirty will be fine." Brigid smiled as she let out a silent breath of relief.

"All right, I'll be there. Should I bring anything?"

"No. I have it all covered." Brigid tried to keep her excitement at bay but began not to care if she did or not.

"Fine, I'll see you then."

"Okay, night, Sam."

"Good night, Brigid."

Chapter Thirty

BRIGID RAN AROUND THE kitchen trying to get everything ready. The steaks were marinating for the grill, the red potatoes roasted in the oven, the fresh string beans tossed in the skillet to sauté, and she was grating the Parmesan cheese for the Caesar salad. Sam was due any second and Brigid wanted everything set before she arrived.

The doorbell rang. *Damn, she's on time.* Artemis sniffed the bottom of the front door and barked twice. Brigid washed and dried her hands before making a dash for the door. She worried that Sam would change her mind before she got to it.

Brigid pushed Artemis away from the door and opened it to find Sam standing on the porch, looking as beautiful as Brigid remembered. Sam had put on some weight since she went into the hospital, but she looked healthier without the gauntness she had before. Her hair was a golden glow of highlights in the early evening sunlight and her lips were soft and firm, begging Brigid to reach up and kiss them. But there was no sparkle in her eyes. Brigid's heart almost broke for her.

Artemis jumped as high as she could to get to Sam's face and lick it. Sam bent down to allow the dog to give her a proper greeting.

"She missed you," Brigid said.

Sam looked at her, a quizzical look on her face.

"I figured out you two have already met, several times I suspect. She's been looking for you in the woods every chance she gets."

"I'm sorry. I know I can't say that enough to make up for what I've done, but I am. Please don't blame Artemis. She is a good watchdog. I don't know why she didn't warn you about me."

"Why don't you come make yourself comfortable out on the deck? I just have to grill the steaks, and then dinner will be ready."

Neither of them spoke while she cooked the meat on the grill. The silence was overwhelming, but Brigid didn't know how to begin. Once the food was done, they sat at the outside table eating and talking. They talked about the weather, and Janet, David, and the kids. Brigid told Sam what had been happening at the bookstore while Sam was gone, including that some of the customers asked for her.

After dinner they cleaned up the dishes and loaded the dishwasher together. Back outside, darkness had fallen, and the moon was rising over the treetops. Brigid could hear the crickets and cicadas in the woods. *How do I do this? Where do I begin such a huge conversation? Maybe I should start in on the most important thing first.*

"Sam, do you love me?" Brigid blurted out, looking deep into Sam's eyes.

"More than I could have ever imagined. I never thought I would love someone the way I love you, Brigid." Sam broke their gaze and looked down at the tabletop. "My whole life I didn't think I would ever find love. It was never something for me. I wasn't able to feel it. Then you came into my life and it happened."

"Sam, do you really mean that, or are you saying it to get out of trouble? I need to know the truth." Brigid felt her life hang in the balance of the answer.

"I mean it, Brigid, with all my heart it's the truth. If you want to press charges, you can. I won't fight it. But it won't change my feelings for you."

"What I want is to know I can trust you. Ever since we talked in the hospital, you have been distant, pushing me away, avoiding me every time I tried to talk to you or get close to you. Why?"

"I don't know why." Tears began forming in Sam's eyes. "I thought you deserved better. Better than someone who can't give you anything right now. Hell, I don't know if I'll ever be able to."

"I don't want anything from you, Sam, except you, your love, and for me to be able to love you back. That's all we need right now." Tears rolled down Brigid's face.

"Do you hear how naïve that all sounds, Brigid? This is not something that can be swept away by love. It is a lifelong illness that will take a long time to even get under control."

"I know that. I've talked to Janet about it and you. I realize the ramifications."

"I don't think you do. I can become a burden, a liability. I could even revert back to the way I was."

"I don't believe that you will, Sam."

"No, it's obvious you don't. The only way I can think to explain it to you is for you to come with me to my next doctor's appointment. Maybe when she tells you, you'll begin to believe me. I'm too much of a burden for you right now, Brigid."

"Let me be the judge of that. I'm capable of deciding who I want in my life on my own. I don't need you to determine this for me."

"Then come with me. Let the doctor tell you what it's like to be me, to be with someone like me."

"Fine, tell me what time and where to meet you and I'll be there. But let me warn you, Sam. Nothing she says is going to scare me away. I love you and nothing is going to change that.

Ellen Hoil

Chapter Thirty-one

BRIGID FOLLOWED THE NURSE to the Doctor's office. As she came in, she saw Sam was already there bouncing her right leg in a nervous manner. As soon as she saw her, Sam made room for her on the couch.

"Thanks for coming," Sam said in a quiet voice.

"Hi, Brigid. I'm Dr. Winski."

Brigid sat next to Sam, so their legs were touching. She took comfort in the contact and hoped Sam did as well. Sam's leg had slowed, though it didn't completely stop.

"So, Samantha was telling me that you're a friend of hers and you want to know more about what was going on with her. Since Samantha has consented, I'll allow you to sit in and hear what we have to say today. You may ask me any questions you might have. Right now, let's start with Samantha. How are you doing today?"

"Better than the other day, I think. I don't feel quite as irritable or antsy." Sam wiped the palms of her hands on her jeans.

"Did you figure out what set you off the other day?"

"I think it was the kids. I think when they get all noisy and out of control like that, the noise and chaos gets to me, along with the stress of feeling responsible for them and what they're doing."

"I see. Is there any way you can get away from them when they are like that? Maybe tell Janet you can't babysit, or go outside for a while?"

"I think Janet would understand about the babysitting, but the house is so small there's no way I can get away from it. I can still hear it in my room. Maybe if I went for a walk it might help."

"Is there someone else you can stay with? I'd rather you not live alone at this point in your treatment, so is there any hope of an alternative?"

"No, not really. I don't know anyone else in town." Sam leaned forward, her hands loosely clasped and her shoulders slumped. "I guess I'll just have to learn to deal with it."

"You could move in with me," Brigid said after a moment of silence.

"No. I won't do it, Brigid."

"Why not? It would be nice and quiet, and you could help keep Artemis out of trouble during the day. I don't see where there could be a problem."

"Because, I won't put you through that. You're here today to find out what a mess I am. You have no idea what kind of problems you're asking for by taking me in. It's not an easy thing to do, Brigid."

"Samantha has a valid point." Dr. Winski interrupted. "Janet understood the ramifications and difficulties of this disorder when she agreed to allow Samantha to stay with her. I wouldn't feel comfortable putting Samantha into an unknown situation. Not unless you fully understand what Samantha's disorder is and what she's going through to get it stabilized."

"Well, then explain it to me," Brigid said.

"May I ask what kind of relationship you have with Samantha? Is it a romantic one?"

"Yes, it is," Brigid said.

Sam was staring past the doctor and out the window. The day was overcast and seemed to match her mood.

"That makes things a little better, but also more difficult for both of you," Dr. Winski said.

"I don't understand," Brigid said.

"If you have a strong relationship it will go a long way in helping you cope with the situation." Dr. Winski leaned forward in her chair. "Samantha, you will have someone to rely on and support you, and you both can be there for each other to help you get through the difficult times. And there will be difficult times, especially in the beginning."

"What do you mean?" Brigid looked between Sam and the doctor. Sam wouldn't meet her eyes.

"There will be issues that arise, some big, some minor. How you deal with them depends on your commitment to each other and to Samantha's recovery.

"For instance, right now Samantha's condition will interfere with her ability to work or hold a job. Working is a stress she can't handle right now. It explains why she left her last job. She may never be able to hold that kind of job again, or any job, depending on how much stress it causes her. Over seventy-percent of people with Bi-polar Disorder are unemployed."

Brigid looked at Sam. Sam was sweating and pale, her hands were trembling. Brigid fought off the urge to take her hand and turned her attention back to the doctor.

"Could she do what she was doing at the bookstore? Helping out when she feels like it?" Brigid asked.

"That will be fine in the future, but right now I don't think Samantha is ready. She just got out of the hospital and we're still trying to get her stable. I know she had some sociability issues when she first arrived in town and I think that right now any kind of large social environment isn't good for her."

"You mean I can't do anything? I have to just sit around all day and do nothing?" Sam asked.

"Not nothing, Samantha. You need to spend this time learning your body and mind. You need to find out what stresses you, what triggers your episodes, and learn how to eliminate them or deal with them. I suggest learning meditation skills or anything else that can help you relax."

"The medications may affect Samantha's mental or physical activity level. Many anti-depressants, especially those effecting serotonin, can cause sleepiness, fatigue, and difficulty focusing. Other drugs have other side effects, which can cause problems." Dr. Winski held up a hand to forestall any comments and leaned back in her chair. "However, we now have Samantha on a combination that I feel will give her the least side effects. But you must understand that a medication can sometimes stop working the way we want it and will have to be changed, or side effects will suddenly appear."

"So, we may never find a good combination of medications for me?"

"No, Samantha. I am saying what can happen. This is a process, one without an exact science. Each person's body is different, and the chemical balance of the brain is unique. We need to find the right combination for you. That may happen with this combination we are trying now, or it may take some time. There is no certainty. That is one of the issues that can cause both of you problems."

"How?" Brigid asked.

"Until we get the right combination of meds for Samantha, she will be subject to mood changes. She can be depressed or manic. If she is rapid cycling it can be hours, days, or weeks between periods. It is not inconceivable for her to be depressed or manic or stable for extended time periods." Dr. Winski sighed. "I can't emphasize or even repeat this enough to both of you. This is not a disorder that is easy to gain or keep control of."

"Will this be forever?" Brigid asked.

"Until we get her stabilized on the right cocktail of drugs, it will continue." Dr. Winski looked at Sam and smiled. "But once we get that figured out, it should stop happening as often. Samantha could go for long periods between episodes and live a normal life along the way. But it is a lifelong disorder. You need to recognize that. It can manifest itself to some degree at any time, whether she is on medication or not."

"Explain what else there is, Dr. Winski. You know that's not all there is." Sam let out a deep sigh.

"Brigid, you will be taking on the role of a caregiver. That alone can be tough on a relationship, especially a new one."

"How so?"

"There is going to be a tendency to want to treat her on a somewhat unequal level," Dr. Winski said.

"I would never do that," Brigid said.

"You may not do it consciously, but I have seen it happen to other couples. You might begin to see her as someone who needs taking care of or protecting, not as a partner."

"What's the best way to avoid that?"

"Brigid, I suggest finding a support group or therapist of your own. That will help you work through many of the issues and, if need be, either your therapist, or Samantha's, can see you as a couple to help you work out issues you may have."

"I can do that. What else do I need to know about?"

"The other major issues can be commitment and sex."

"Commitment and sex...what are you talking about?" Brigid looked at Samantha.

Samantha blushed and looked to the doctor.

"What I mean is that most Bi-polar individuals have a hard time with commitment and follow through. They will start projects but not finish them, begin jobs and then quit. Start new relationships and end them. Bi-polar people can lose interest easily. Samantha has shown some signs of this, but nothing on a major level that should concern you. Also, if she is like most of my patients she may try and push you away to avoid being a burden."

"Okay," Brigid said, confident that she and Sam could avoid that issue. "But what about sex? How does that play a role in all this?"

"A major symptom of some manic episodes is an unhealthy increase in sexual drive. Depending on how severe the episode, the need for sex becomes almost an addiction. However, during a depressive episode, the desire for sex may disappear altogether, and some of the medications Samantha takes may interfere with her sexual drive. But we are trying ones with very few side effects, so hopefully that won't be a problem."

Sam's blush deepened. "Samantha has told me about some thoughts she has had in the past and recently that make me think that you and she could run into some other issues." Dr. Winski once again leaned forward.

"What kind of issues?" Brigid said.

"Much of her recent behavior toward you has been an attempt to distance herself from her desires, combined with a feeling of low self-image at this point. This may improve over time, but it may become a completely opposite situation should she become manic."

"I don't understand." Brigid's eyebrows knitted together.

"Samantha could fall into the idea of a sexual relationship with you easier than it should be since she is being driven by her illness rather than her true emotions. As I said, one of the most common symptoms of Bi-polar disorder is a high sex drive. Samantha may find herself desiring sexual relations with you just because of that rather than out of her normal emotions. It doesn't mean she doesn't respect you, or have less feelings for you as a person, but it could happen."

"Wow, that's a lot to take in," Brigid said, overwhelmed. She looked at Sam, who was bright red and wouldn't meet her glance.

"What you have to remember, Brigid, is that this is a lifelong illness. You both have to make adjustments in your lives if you want this relationship to work." Dr. Winski looked at Sam. "You also need to keep in mind the amount of strength and courage it takes for someone to learn to live with this illness. I have no doubts that once we find the right combination of meds, you and Samantha will be able to adjust just fine."

Brigid took Sam's cold and clammy hand in hers. "Neither do I." Brigid squeezed Sam's hand.

Chapter Thirty-two

AFTER LEAVING THE DOCTOR'S office, Brigid and Sam went back to her house. Artemis had been sad ever since Sam left the night before and Brigid thought it a good idea to give them some playtime.

Brigid called Janet at work and asked her to stop on her way home. Since she didn't know how long she and Janet's talk would last, Brigid made lasagna for Janet to take home to David and the twins. She also made one for her and Samantha to share. As she was taking the food out of the oven, she heard Janet call her from the front hallway.

"In the kitchen," Brigid yelled.

"Wow, something smells good in here."

"I made dinner for everyone. There's a tray here for you to take home." Brigid pointed to the food cooling on the stovetop.

"Have I ever told you how much I love you?" Janet gave her a hug with one arm.

"No, you never have," Brigid teased back.

"Well, I do, so there," Janet said, sticking her tongue out at Brigid. Janet let her sister go and walked over to the sliding glass door. "She seems happier today, especially out there playing."

Brigid looked past Janet to see Sam running around laughing at the dog's antics. "Yeah, she does."

"She looks relaxed, more relaxed than she has in some time. I'm sure you have a lot to do with that, Brigid"

"I don't know about that, but she does seem to be relieving some stress out there."

Sam turned and waved. She threw the ball one more time into the woods before heading for the house. Janet opened the door, stepping outside to meet her.

"Hi, Samantha." Janet reached out and pulled her into a hug.

"Hey, Janet. How was work today?"

"Nothing major." Janet sat at the patio table and Sam sat across from her. "How did your meeting with the doctor go today?" Janet asked, as Brigid joined them. Brigid put her hand on Sam's shoulder, giving it a gentle squeeze before sitting next to her.

Sam's eyes lit up as she looked at Brigid. She told Janet about the appointment, with Brigid interjecting a comment once in a while.

"Are you sure you're okay with this, Samantha?" Janet asked.

"Yeah, I think so. You know I love the twins, but they're too much stress for me to take on a constant basis. The house is too small, and the noise and activity level are too high," Sam said with an apologetic look.

"I understand. Sometimes it's too much for me to handle and they're my kids." Janet chuckled.

"This is the best solution, Janet," Brigid said. "The doctor doesn't want her to be living alone right at the moment. It's quiet here. She can play with Artemis, or walk to town, and I'll be home in the evenings. Melissa or Stan can cover evenings at the store. Stan wants more time since his college classes are over for now."

"Are you sure you can handle this, Brigid? What if Samantha has an episode like she did the other day?"

"Truthfully, I don't know. But I think I can do it. I won't know until, or if, it happens. I have the doctor's number in case of emergency, and you live five minutes away if I need help."

"I think you can both do it. I've haven't seen you this happy in years, Brigid, and Samantha, you seem to be calm here. I know you two will be strong together. When do you want to move in?"

"I think it's best to do it as soon as possible. I'd rather not have a repeat of the other night. I think it scared me a little more than I was prepared for. I'm sorry."

"Samantha, please don't apologize for things you have no control over," Janet said.

"Sure, Sam. Let's do it tomorrow," Brigid said. "We can grab your stuff from Janet's. The rest of it is at my place. I hope you don't mind, but I didn't know what else to do with it. Why don't you stay here tonight? I have some sweats you can sleep in and we can throw your clothes in the wash before we go to bed."

Sam looked at her as they stood just inside the doorway and placed her hand over Brigid's. "Are you sure, Brigid? I don't want to put you out."

"You're not putting me out. We're going to move you into the guest room anyway. What's one day early? We picked up your scripts at the pharmacy, so you're okay there."

"I think she's right, Samantha." Janet nodded. "I think you'll be fine here."

"Okay, I'll stay." Sam looked from Brigid to Janet and back to Brigid.

"Great," Brigid said, happiness overwhelming her at the thought of finally having Sam close by.

"Well, now that we've settled that, I think I'll head home. Thanks for making dinner," giving Brigid a kiss on the top of her head, "It will be nice to have time for dinner with the kids and David without the hassle of having to cook around them all."

"I'll carry the lasagna out to the car for you, Janet," Sam said, turning and leaving the two alone.

Janet looked at her sister as Brigid watched Sam walk outside. "You know you can call me anytime if you have any trouble or questions, or if you just want to talk to someone."

"I know."

"Really, Brigid. Don't hesitate to call, anytime day or night."

"I will, I promise." Brigid kissed Janet on the cheek as Janet pulled her into a hug.

Brigid stood in the doorway and watched Janet climb into the car as Sam held the door for her and closed it behind her. As Janet drove away, Sam stood in the driveway looking at the retreating car. The setting sun silhouetted her in its golden glow as it turned the skies various hues of pink, purple, and dark blue. Brigid thought about how the blue matched Samantha's eyes.

Brigid thought about the visit to the doctor earlier in the day and all that she learned. It would be a long road ahead of them, but she knew, deep in her heart, that they would find the strength to face whatever befell them.

Brigid watched as Sam turned and began walking toward her. Brigid's heart filled with the beauty and strength she saw before her. She held out her hand.

"Come on, honey. Let's have dinner together." *Hopefully this is only the beginning.*

Ellen Hoil

Chapter Thirty-three

IT TOOK THE TWO women most of the day, but by early the following evening Sam and Brigid had moved most of Sam's stuff into Brigid's house. Sam insisted on bringing most of her books and Brigid agreed to turn her extra room into a small library for Sam.

While Brigid made dinner, Sam assembled the books into neat piles. Brigid came in and watched as Sam went through the book titles and put them in some sort of order. From what Brigid could see, they were not sorted alphabetically or by topic. It appeared random to her, but it must have made some sense to Sam since she was so meticulous about the process. When dinner was ready, they sat down to eat. The conversation all day had been polite and civil, but stilted. The dinner conversation was no different. In fact, conversation was almost non-existent. Eventually the quiet got to be too much for Brigid.

"Do you think you're getting settled in?"

Sam looked up with a surprised stare. Sam looked over her shoulder for a split second, seeming to check that it was she that Brigid was talking to. "Uhm, fine, I guess. I put my clothes in the guest room and started putting the books away in the spare room. I hope that's all right."

Brigid sighed. "Sam, this is your place now too. You can put your stuff wherever it makes you comfortable. I want you to feel at home here."

"Oh, okay," Sam said a little sheepishly.

Brigid began gathering the empty plates.

"I'll do that," Sam said as she took the plates from her. "It's the least I can do since you cooked dinner."

"All right, how about from now on whoever cooks the other does the dishes? Sound fair?" Brigid raised an eyebrow.

"Yeah," Sam said.

"After you're done, do you want to watch some TV or a movie or something?"

"I don't know. I have to take my meds soon and that usually wipes me out pretty fast."

"Well, why don't you take your pills and we'll pick out a movie. If you get tired you can go to bed. I don't want you to feel like you need to lock yourself in your room, Sam. You need to make this your home, and you can't do that if you think you have to stay out of my way all the time."

"Sure, that would be great."

***

Brigid sorted through her video collection while Sam went upstairs to her room. As she entered the room her nervous tension returned. The room felt too small. Beads of sweat formed on her upper lip. Even though she tried to calm herself, her breathing increased.

I don't understand why I'm so uncomfortable. Maybe it's because this might end any minute? Once Brigid realizes what is involved, I feel like she'll give up on us even though she said she loves me and is willing to stick by me. Why can't I believe that? Why can't I have more faith in us?

Sam pulled her pill bottles out of the medicine cabinet Brigid had put in her room and took a pill from each bottle, and then washed them down with one gulp of water. She took several moments getting herself together by taking deep breaths and massaging the back of her neck. Finally, she felt well enough to head downstairs. As she came down the stairs, she saw Brigid's profile as she looked through various DVD cases. Sam took in the beauty of the woman she loved, the woman who loved her. *I still can't believe that she has forgiven me for all I did to her. What did I ever do to deserve the love of a woman like her? Nothing, that's what, but I promise to make her happy for the rest of my life.*

***

Brigid turned around when she heard Sam's footsteps on the stairs. She stood up and admired the way the light in the upstairs hallway made Sam seem almost ethereal. Brigid knew Sam had doubts about them, but Brigid was willing to do almost anything to make Sam realize their destiny lay together. She met Sam, who seemed frozen in spot, at the bottom of the stairs. Brigid took her hand and led her to the sofa in front of the television.

"I picked out a nice comedy, figuring we could both go for a little humor. Do you want some microwave popcorn?"

"Sure, if you want," Sam said.

"Okay, I'll be right back. Why don't you put the movie in?"

Brigid went into the kitchen and, as she popped the popcorn, thought about Sam's behavior since she agreed to move in. *She's so unlike the person I knew at the store, so unsure of herself. How did she become different? She had her quirks, but she was so self-assured. Now she seems to question everything she does and says. I hope it's only temporary and we can get her back to being herself again.*

Brigid came back into the room and took a seat in the corner of the couch. Sam sat down in the other corner and pulled her feet up under her and wrapped her arms around herself as the movie started. Brigid could see the sense of desolation Sam was experiencing. Brigid moved to the middle of the couch and, with a gentle "come here," pulled Sam over to lay her head on her lap. She felt Sam relax as Brigid trickled her fingers through Sam's hair. Sam's breathing slowed and soon Brigid felt her fall asleep.

Brigid let the movie play, but she watched Sam sleep instead of the screen. Asleep, the tension and anxiety were gone, replaced by serenity.

***

Sam woke up to the late morning light shining in her eyes. A little disoriented, it took her a moment to realize that she had slept on the couch. There was no sign of Brigid, but a blanket had been placed over her sometime during the night.

When she was awake enough to get up, she wandered into the kitchen for some tea. As she crossed the kitchen to the electric kettle, she noticed Brigid had set everything out for her. She turned on the kettle, and liking her teas extra strong some days, she put three tea bags in the cup, and stood watching the pot.

"You know what they say about a watched pot," Brigid said behind her.

Sam jumped and turned around. "I thought you went to work." She held her hand to her chest.

"Nah, I decided to go in late."

"Why?" Sam had a feeling she was the reason and she wasn't sure how she felt about that fact.

"No real reason. After being off last night I felt like being a little lazy, so I took the morning off too."

Sam felt the real reason was to keep an eye on her.

"How did you sleep? I know you said you were fine on the couch, but I was worried you would be uncomfortable."

Sam had no recollection of the conversation. "Great, except I can't believe I fell asleep on you."

"That couch can be very cozy to sleep on. I've done it myself a time or two," Brigid grabbed a pan off the stove. "Would you like some eggs for breakfast?"

"Sure. Scrambled would be nice, thanks."

"You seem a lot more relaxed today. Maybe since you slept so well?"

"I hope so." It had been a long time since Sam had a home cooked meal with someone special to her. Not since her parents died had she felt like this. It felt like home.

"I've got an appointment with my therapist. When I get back, I'm going to oil that squeaky closet door and see what else needs to be done."

"You don't have to do that," Brigid said.

"I want to. It will make me feel useful for a change."

As Brigid prepared to leave for work, she walked around the table to where Sam was sitting. She bent down and kissed Sam on her lips. It was meant to be a chaste goodbye kiss. However, as their lips met Sam marveled at the feel of Brigid's lips on her own. She deepened the kiss to one full of love and tenderness. Brigid responded to the change. Sam felt fingers caress the nape of her neck and begin playing with the fringe of hair there. Sam put a hand behind Brigid's head and pulled her deeper still. As tongues met, Brigid moaned far in the back of her throat. Sam moved her hand inside Brigid's shirt. Upon realizing what she was doing, she pulled back, as if burned.

"We can't do this, Brigid. Not now," Sam said with regret in her voice.

"I know. We can finish this later, when I get home."

"No, Brigid, I mean we can't do this at all. It wouldn't be right, for either of us."

"What are you talking about? How can it not be right? We love each other. Tell me you truly meant it, Sam."

"Of course, I meant every word. But don't you see this is exactly why we can't? You still doubt me, who I am. And I have no confidence in myself or my emotions or what I have to offer you."

"No, I don't see. Together we have the power to help each other with all of that. Just give it some time and you'll see. It will work itself out."

"I don't see, Brigid. I don't see how we can build a relationship based on mistrust and cowardice." Sam took a deep breath, trying to calm herself down. She was on the edge of being out of control—her palms were beginning to sweat, and her anger was rising. "Look, all I am saying is let's put the physical relationship on the back burner for now. I think we both have enough to think about and worry over without adding physical intimacy into it. How can we be intimate with all these things overshadowing us?"

"How can we not be? This is when we need each other the most, when we need our love for each other to help us be strong."

Sam got up and pulled Brigid into a hug, wrapping her arms tightly around her. Brigid immediately put her face in the crook of her neck. Sam could feel her breathing in the scent of her, while Sam reveled in the feeling of comfort and contentment. Sam rested her chin on the top of Brigid's head.

"Sweetheart, can you honestly say, deep down in your mind, not your heart, that you really know me? That you understand me and how I think?"

Brigid took a minute to answer. "No," Brigid answered in a small quiet whisper.

Sam held on to her tighter as she felt the tears moisten her neck and shoulder. Her heart broke at the thought that she had once again caused Brigid pain and a single tear of her own made its way down her cheek.

"It's okay, honey, sssshhh, I promise it'll be all right. It's just for a little while. Only until we get settled. Then we can see how it goes from there. I'm sure before too long we'll be right where we both want to be right now," Sam said, laying a kiss on the top of Brigid's head.

"Do you promise?"

"Yeah, I promise," Sam said, sitting back down and pulling Brigid onto her lap and wrapping her arms tightly around her waist. Brigid laid her head on Sam's shoulder. They would work through this, Sam knew. "All I'm saying, love, is that we not let things get out of hand. We need to take it slow for a while, until we are both comfortable."

"We can still do this though, right?"

"I hoped you would feel that way. I just want to hold off on the sex aspect of our relationship until we feel on equal footing."

"I can agree with you about that. Maybe we should wait. But just know it won't change the way I feel about you, and I intend on letting that show every day."

"All right, deal. So long as you know that I do truly love you and cherish you," Sam said.

"I do," Brigid said.

Chapter Thirty-four

IT HAD BEEN TWO weeks since Sam and Brigid had agreed to take their relationship slow. So far, it was working out. They showed affection and tenderness to one another but spent a lot of time talking and getting to know each other again. For Brigid it was wonderful discovering that the person she knew before was still a part of Sam. She could see that Sam was becoming more comfortable in her surroundings and with herself. Sam spent her days taking care of things around the house, shopping, and playing with Artemis. Brigid was beginning to suspect the dog liked Sam better than her since the dog never left Sam's side. Artemis had even begun to sleep with her at night.

"Are you sure you're up for going to the bookstore, Sam? You know the doctor didn't want you to overstress yourself."

"No, it'll be fine, I promise. I'll just sit around and read some. If I feel any pressure or unease, I'll come home." Sam kissed Brigid lightly on the lips.

"Okay, but only since you promised so nicely," Brigid said with a laugh.

"Well, I do promise. I need to start getting out. I feel like I've been away from the world for months. Between the hospital, and then Janet's, and now being stuck here, I am about at my wit's end."

"You don't really feel stuck here, do you, Sam?"

"No, of course not, I mean that I feel cooped up. I guess it's a case of cabin fever. Once I get out and about, I'll feel fine again. I need some fresh air and new surroundings. I love it here with you." She pulled Brigid into a deep kiss. Once they broke for much needed air, she smiled at her. "I love you and our home."

Brigid had to swallow past the lump in her throat when Sam referred to it as their home. "I love that you're here with me too, and I love you more than I think you realize sometimes."

"Maybe, but either way we have to get going. The store isn't going to run itself." Sam gave Brigid one last gentle squeeze before letting her go.

Sam spent most of the day sitting in the main area reading a book and helping out at the counter when she could. Several people came up to her during the day to ask how she was. Overall, she felt comfortable.

Sam was reading when a shadow fell across her book. She looked up to see Michele Blake, her nurse from the hospital.

"Hi, Samantha," Michele said.

"Hi."

"How have you been?"

"Okay, I guess, at least for the most part."

"I hope everything is better for you now."

"Yeah, it is better. I moved in with my friend that you met at the hospital."

"Ah, Brigid. I remember," Michele said with a knowing twinkle in her eye and a small grin on her face. "She owns the store, right?"

"Yeah, she does," Samantha said.

"So how are you two doing together?"

"We are doing well. Settling into a nice routine, though today is my first day here."

"How are you doing? Are you having a nice time of it?"

"Yeah, so far everyone's been great."

Sam wasn't sure what she expected. Being in public for the first time, she sometimes felt as if she had a big sign on her forehead saying, "Mentally Ill Person." She wondered if that feeling would ever go away and was a little disconcerted by the idea that it wouldn't.

"I'm glad to hear that. I'm happy you're settling in and feeling better."

"I am. I think. Brigid and Janet have been really helpful. They've supported me through everything."

"That's great, Samantha. I hope everything keeps going your way," Michele said with a sincere smile. "I'll let you get back to your book. I just wanted to step over and say hello."

"Thanks, Michele. I'm glad I got to see you again. It's sort of nice to know you've seen me in a period of normalcy," Samantha said, looking up into the friendly face. "It was sort of awkward leaving there with people thinking about me the way I was."

"We never thought badly of you, Samantha. All of us know how these things work. No one believes you were anything other than a nice person in a bad situation over which you never had any control. In the end, you proved to be a very strong person."

"Thanks. That means a great deal to me."

"Well, it's the truth, believe that."

"I'll try," Sam promised, with a small grin.

"Good, well, I have to get going. I'm due at work soon."

"Okay. Thanks for stopping by and for saying what you did."

"It was my pleasure, Samantha. 'Bye."

As Michele put her book on the counter, Sam watched Brigid look up and be surprised to see who stood there. Brigid looked over toward Sam, who gave her a brief nod. Michele said something that made Brigid smile a broad smile. Sam could see her eyes sparkle from where she sat as Brigid looked at her again and then back at Michele, to whom she said something that made the nurse laugh. Sam knew she was the topic of conversation, but she didn't mind. In their own way, both were special to her.

After Michele left the store, Sam watched as Brigid made her way to her. God, she's beautiful. The love of her life stood beside her chair, resting her hip against its side.

"How did that go? Are you okay?" Brigid put her hand on Sam's shoulder and ran a caressing finger over the skin exposed by her shirt collar.

"Yeah, I'm fine. It was nice seeing her like this." Sam took hold of the wandering fingers and placed them against her cheek. "Really, it's okay. I sort of missed her when I got out of the hospital. She was a big part of my life in there."

"She comes in here once in a while, so you can still talk to her when she does." Brigid gazed into Sam's eyes. They stared at each other for several moments. Finally, Sam couldn't take it anymore and gave the hand she was holding a gentle pull and drew Brigid to her lips. The kiss they shared was gentle and tender, but each knew the promise of passion it held. One day they would be able to express it completely.

Ellen Hoil

Chapter Thirty-five

THE EARLY FALL WEATHER was lovely, and Brigid decided to walk home. But the trip wasn't as pleasant as the walk in. That morning, Sam was with her, and Brigid recalled the enjoyment of holding hands as they made their way to town.

She used the serenity the walk home now provided to reflect on the times she and Sam had shared over the last few months. For the most part things had gone well. Sam was as stable now as she had ever been. Both of them were in therapy, and Sam had even found a support group in the area.

There was some trouble early on, as Dr. Winski had predicted. Brigid became a little overprotective and Sam pushed back, angry and sullen. But they worked through it and Brigid learned there was a difference between loving someone, protecting and caring for them, and being overprotective to the point of suffocating.

However, there had been some incidents before Sam's medication was adjusted and one in particular had scared Brigid.

Brigid and Sam walked into the house after a long day at the store and Artemis, as usual, was excited to see them. After a cursory greeting to Brigid, the dog begged Sam to go outside to play for a while. Brigid was excited to be home since David had come by and installed bookcases in the spare room for Sam. Sam went outside with the dog and Brigid went upstairs to see the results of the work.

The room was marvelous. High oak bookcases lined three of the walls. They were lightly stained to allow the natural color and grain to shine through. Brigid wanted to surprise her by having it all set up when she came in, so, rather than starting dinner, she began putting the numerous books on the shelves. She had been at it for almost an hour when Sam came into the room.

"Wow, they're beautiful." The next moment Sam raced over and ripped the book Brigid was holding out of her hand. "What are

you doing?" she screamed.

"I was putting the books away. Don't you like the bookcases?"

"I don't care about the damn cases. What are you doing with my books? You're ruining everything.,"

"Sam, calm down. I was just arranging them."

"No, don't you see? You messed them all up...they were already arranged. Now I'm going to have to spend hours going through them all because you couldn't keep your God damn hands out of my stuff."

"Honey, I was just trying to make it nice, to surprise you with. What's the matter?"

"What's the matter is you're touching my stuff. I can't get even a little privacy around here. You're always here, always nosing around me." Sam became more agitated with each word. By the time she finished she was irate, her face red with anger, her body shaking.

Brigid hadn't seen her like this since the day in the motel room. She tried to remain calm, though her heartbeat raced. "I'm sorry you feel that way, Sam. I promise I'll try to give you more space, if that's what you need," she said, as she held up her hands.

"It's too fucking late for that, Brigid. You've already done the damage."

Sam began knocking over the remaining piles of books, throwing some across the room.

"Sam! Please stop," Brigid pleaded.

Sam seemed to tire herself out. She stopped and looked around, breathing in heavy gasps.

Brigid took a step toward her, but Sam recoiled, moving quickly in the opposite direction.

"Just leave me alone," she said with irritation in her voice and something Brigid didn't recognize.

"Sweetheart—"

"No, just leave me alone," Sam said in a quiet, tired voice. "Please, Brigid, just leave me alone." Sam turned and walked out of the room.

Brigid heard the door to Sam's room slam. She saw that there was no light coming through the slit at the bottom of the door.

Brigid went back downstairs and called Janet "Janet, it's about Sam. I think I need help."

"Okay, take a deep breath and tell me what happened."

Brigid told her everything that happened that night. "I don't know why she went off. What should I do? I can't leave her like this, she might hurt herself. I have to do something, don't I?"

"Calm down, Brigid. How was she at the store? Did she seem short or irritable?"

"She did appear to be a little reserved. She didn't talk much to anybody all day."

"It sounds like she may have been feeling unwell all day. Don't take what happened personally, Brigid."

"Okay, but what do I do now?" Brigid gripped the phone harder, her knuckles turning white.

"Call her doctor. Tell her what you told me. Can you do that?"

"Yeah, I'll do that right now."

"All right, I'm coming over. By then you should be hearing back from someone at the office."

"Right, I'll call as soon as we hang up."

"I'm coming. Don't worry, Brigid. We'll take care of this."

Brigid hung up and called the doctor's office. She got the answering service and left a message for someone to call her back. Looking for something to do while she waited, she put the electric kettle on for tea so she and Janet could have a cup when she got there. Brigid sat and waited for something to happen. She heard the front door open at the same time the phone rang. Grabbing the phone off the hook, she was relieved to hear Dr. Winski on the other end. She gave the doctor the details of the evening and how Sam had been during the day.

"I was afraid of this when you decided to let Samantha go back to the store. But don't worry, it is easily fixed," Dr. Winksi said. "Do you know if Samantha took her pills tonight?"

"I don't know for sure. She usually takes them before bed."

"See if you can get her to take her regular pills and an extra dose of the Klonopin. Call me if you need me to talk to her. I'll give you my emergency number."

Brigid wrote down the number. "Thank you, Dr. Winski, for getting back to me so fast."

"No problem, Brigid. Let me know if you need more help. Please call tomorrow morning for an appointment. I want to see both of you."

After she hung up, Brigid filled Janet in with what the doctor said.

"Do you want me to take care of this?" Janet asked.

"No. I need to learn to deal with these things," Brigid said in a voice that sounded more confident than she felt. "I'll go."

Brigid went up the stairs to Sam's room. She tried the door and was grateful to find it unlocked. The room was dark, with only a slit of moonlight coming in through the window. Samantha was lying on the bed, her face hidden in the pillow. Sam's body was rigid, her muscles so tight they trembled.

Brigid went to the medicine cabinet and began pulling out bottles, trying to read the labels in the dim light. She found the ones she needed and grabbed a bottle of water. She sat on the edge of the bed.

"Sam?"

"Go away. Please, Brigid."

"No, Sam, I'm not leaving. Here, I got your pills for you. Please, take them. They will make you feel better."

Sam lay there for several minutes, neither moving nor saying anything. At last, Sam turned her head and reached for the pills. She threw them in her mouth and swallowed them down with a swig of water. She laid back down and faced away from Brigid.

"You can go now, Brigid. I'll be fine. I'm just tired."

"That's okay. I'll just stay until you fall asleep." Brigid put a hand on the small of Sam's back and felt her tense at her touch.

"I'm sorry, Brigid. I ruined everything."

"You didn't ruin anything. We'll spend time tomorrow fixing everything. We can talk in the morning, and then you can spend the rest of the day arranging the books anyway you want," she said.

"Brigid, can I ask you something?"

"Sure, honey."

"Why do you love me? I have so many problems. Why do you want me around?"

The light from the window reflected on Sam's face. Brigid saw the tears running down Sam's nose.

"I want you here because I love you." Brigid laid down beside her and took her in her arms. "And I love you because I know you are a beautiful person inside and out."

Brigid felt Sam stiffen, but she didn't stop. "I love you because of the person you are. I thought for a while I would never see that person again, but I have. Sam, you are the same wonderful person I fell in love with, even before I was ready to admit it to myself."

"But I'm not the same person. I've changed. I'm sick. I'll never be well again."

"You're right. You're not the same person anymore. You're so much more now. I see that and so will you. I'll show you the person you've become." Brigid pulled her tighter. She began to feel Sam relax and after a few moments, she rolled over and laid her head on Brigid's shoulder, resting it beneath her chin. Brigid took the opportunity to place a gentle kiss on her head.

"I have seen a gentle person who cares about others. One who is outgoing and friendly to everyone she meets. Your strength is amazing. You have fought this illness at every turn, and I know you'll continue to. You have it in you to face this problem head on. I know that, because I know you, Sam, and the person I know is the person I love, with all my heart."

"You deserve better."

"No, I have just what I want and need. I don't deserve better because there is no one better for me."

Brigid lay there and waited to see what Sam would do or say next. But after several minutes of silence she became concerned. Moving so she could see her face, she was relieved to see that Sam was asleep. She made herself comfortable and closed her eyes. She enjoyed the feel of Sam in her arms. It made her feel whole. Complete.

The next morning, they found Janet asleep on the couch. After sending her home, the two discussed what had happened and then spent the afternoon arranging the books in the new library. Sam called Dr. Winski's office and arranged to see her that afternoon.

***

That was the only serious episode Sam had since moving in. Dr. Winski, adjusted her medications and since then she was as stable as any person Brigid knew. She was aware that could change. But they had dealt with it. She was no longer afraid of the unknown.

Brigid walked into the house and was greeted by Artemis and the wondrous aroma of garlic and basil. She called for Sam but got no reply. The dog followed her into the kitchen where she found a pasta and vodka sauce cooking on the stove. She looked in the oven and found fresh garlic bread.

Brigid went into the dining room, looking for Sam. Set on the table was a white linen tablecloth with the china her mother had given her. In the center were two silver candleholders with lavender candles in them. On one of the plates was a note.

"Meet me outside."

Brigid stepped through the sliding doors onto the deck. There she found more candles lined up around the deck, throwing off a gentle light. Sam was laying in one of the Adirondack lounge chairs.

"What is all this?" Brigid asked as she took the glass of white wine Sam offered her.

Sam made a motion for Brigid to join her on the lounge.

"Did you do all this?" Brigid asked as she sat down.

"Yes, though Artemis helped test the pasta and sauce, but the rest I did," Sam said with a big grin on her face.

"Well, I am certainly impressed." Brigid gave her a gentle kiss on the lips to emphasize her point.

Sam stood up and took Brigid by the hand. "Come in and enjoy it before it gets cold."

As they sat down to eat, Brigid asked, "What's the special occasion?"

Sam looked at her with a broad smile. "It's our anniversary."

"Our anniversary? What anniversary?"

"Sort of. It was eight months ago today that we met."

"You remember to the day exactly when we met?" Brigid was shocked since she had trouble remembering her own birthday.

"Yes, I do. It was the most important day of my life. I still remember the cute attempt you made to get me to talk to you. I'm sorry it didn't work sooner."

"I'm not. I'm glad everything worked out the way it did. If anything changed would we be where we are now? I don't know, and I don't want to take that risk."

"I love you, Brigid, and I wanted to let you know how important that is to me. The fact that you came into my life saved me. I will always appreciate that."

"I love you too, Sam, more than I ever thought I would again."

"I'm glad." Sam took one of Brigid's hands and placed a kiss on the palm. "Now eat before this gets cold."

Dinner was a romantic affair. They ate and made quiet conversation about everyday things, but also about what they wanted in the future.

"I want to be with you for the rest of my life, Brigid. To grow old with you by my side. I can't think of any better way to spend the rest of my days but in showing you every day how much I love you and what you mean to me."

After dinner, Sam put the dishes in the sink and joined Brigid in the living room. Brigid had started a fire in the fireplace and placed pillows and a blanket in front of it. The soft jazz sound of Ella Fitzgerald played in the background.

Sam came up behind her as she stood in front of the fire. She wrapped her arms around Brigid's waist, and she whispered, "I want you, Brigid, more than I have ever wanted anything in my whole life." She gently spun Brigid around and kissed her passionately. Their tongues danced around each other in gentle caresses.

Brigid put her hands-on Sam's shoulders before moving down to her chest, stopping just above her breasts. Her own hands made their way under the back of Brigid's shirt, running along the smooth skin of her back. Sam was amazed at the feel of Brigid's warm skin. The supple tenderness of it brushing against her fingers sent stimulating chills through her body.

As they broke the kiss, Brigid began unbuttoning Sam's shirt. But once she had the top two open, Sam reached down and pulled it over her head, surprising Brigid with the fact that she wore no bra. Brigid removed her own shirt and bra. It didn't take long to take off the other's remaining clothing.

***

"My God, you're beautiful," Sam said as she reached out to touch Brigid.

They gasped at the feel of their naked bodies touching. Passion pulsated through Sam's veins, renewing her energy. As they kissed again, Brigid took Sam's breasts in her hands and began kneading them. Sam was loving the feel of them in Brigid's hands. After a few moments she couldn't take it anymore. "Please."

Brigid took a pert nipple into her mouth and rasping her tongue against it. Sam groaned and placed her hand on the back of Brigid's head to encourage her more.

"Brigid, I have to lie down. I can't stand anymore. I don't think I can take much more."

Brigid pulled her to the floor. She straddled her hips and leaned down to kiss her, groaning into her mouth as Sam gave her breasts some attention. Sam was lightheaded from the sensations. Their mounds ground together, mixing their essences, making them each moan into the kiss and deepen it still further, as if they could share their souls through it.

***

Brigid broke the kiss and reached down to stroke between Sam's legs.

"Brigid, my God, I love you so much, please!" Sam called out as she threw her head back.

Brigid's urging body couldn't take anymore; she needed to touch her. Brigid slid two fingers deep into Sam's silky depths. The warm moisture greeted her and increased her desire tenfold as she began to slide her fingers in and out, going back for more over and over again.

"Please Brigid, touch me, I need you, love," Sam begged.

Brigid began rubbing and stroking Sam, using her thumb to bring her to the pinnacle. Sam screamed out her release, "Brigid!" Brigid swallowed the scream with a deep kiss, rubbing herself against Sam's muscular thigh, throwing herself over the edge to join her lover.

***

They spent the rest of the evening on the floor sharing each other. They got to know one another in the most intimate ways only two women could. When they rested between bouts of lovemaking, they made love with their words, planning their future and reveling in the joy they brought each other.

When the sun came up, it found them asleep entwined in each other's arms, Brigid resting her head on Sam's shoulder, an arm wrapped around her mid-section. Sam's arms wrapped protectively around Brigid, holding her close.

When Brigid woke up, she was disoriented until she realized she was sleeping on top of Sam. The feelings and memories of the night before came back to her and she smiled in contentment. She tightened her grip around Sam.

"Good morning," Sam said squeezing Brigid to her body. "Have I told you how much I love you, and how much I am looking forward to waking up every morning for the rest of my life to you?"

Brigid smiled, nestling her head further into the breast on which it laid. "No, not within the last few minutes."

Sam pinched her butt.

"Ow! Hey."

"Then I have been remiss in my duty."

"You've been remiss in nothing. I know how much you love me by the fact that I can barely move." Brigid laughed. "But you have failed to give me a proper good morning greeting." Brigid leaned up and pressed her lips against Sam's. However, what started out as a gentle caress deepened.

Before it could go farther Brigid moved away. "Food, I need food if we are going to keep at this much longer."

"Okay, you go shower and I'll get you some breakfast." Sam kissed her tenderly.

"All right, but remember while I'm gone that I love you beyond measure."

"I will," Sam promised.

Brigid got up and began walking up the stairs, leaving Sam alone.

Sam stood and moved slowly into the kitchen. "I don't think I will ever know what I did to deserve her love, but I plan on spending the rest of my life being worthy of her."

The End

About Ellen Hoil

Ellen Hoil lives in wine country on the North Fork of Long Island between The Sound and The Peconic Bay. "I can't imagine living anywhere that isn't near water and open space." When she isn't writing fiction, she does write for her other career as an in-house counsel attorney.

During her down time Ellen enjoys her hobbies of photography and getting involved in local politics. She is an ardent Sci-Fi geek and can be found at various conventions. "My philosophy on life is that failure is never the end, but only a temporary stopping off point for a new adventure."

Connect with Ellen

Email: e.hoil22@yahoo.com

Facebook: E Hoil Author

Note to Readers:

Thank you for reading a book from Desert Palm Press. We have made every effort to edit this book. However, typos do slip in. If you find an error in the text, please email lee@desertpalmpress.com so the issue can be corrected.

We appreciate you as a reader and want to ensure you enjoy the reading process. We would like you to consider posting a review on your preferred media sites and/or your blog or website.

For more information on upcoming releases, author interviews, contest, giveaways and more, please sign up for our newsletter and visit us as at Desert Palm Press: www.desertpalmpress.com and "Like" us on Facebook: Desert Palm Press.

Bright Blessings

Desert Palm Press

Made in the USA
Middletown, DE
12 June 2021